BEYOND THE MOON AND THE HEARTACHE TOO

ANNE HUTCHESON

BEYOND THE MOON AND THE HEARTACHE TOO

iUniverse books may be ordered through booksellers or by contacting:

iUniverse
1663 Liberty Drive
Bloomington, IN 47403
www.iuniverse.com
1-800-Authors (1-800-288-4677)

*Because of the dynamic nature of the Internet, any web addresses or links contained in
this book may have changed since publication and may no longer be valid. The views
expressed in this work are solely those of the author and do not necessarily reflect the views
of the publisher, and the publisher hereby disclaims any responsibility for them.*

*This is a work of fiction. All of the characters, names, incidents, organizations, and dialogue
in this novel are either the products of the author's imagination or are used fictitiously.*

*Any people depicted in stock imagery provided by Getty Images are models,
and such images are being used for illustrative purposes only.
Certain stock imagery © Getty Images.*

ISBN: 978-1-5320-4936-1 (sc)
ISBN: 978-1-5320-4938-5 (hc)
ISBN: 978-1-5320-4937-8 (e)

Library of Congress Control Number: 2018908748

Print information available on the last page.

iUniverse rev. date: 08/31/2018

For the lonely

Other Titles by Anne Hutcheson

Ill Will
Beauty Full
Winning Wishes

There comes a time in every life
when the world gets quiet and the only
thing left is your own heart.
—Sarah Dessen

1

Sidnei Jewell looked up at the sky and wondered. There was the daytime moon, right on time. It was appearing after the full moon, and the big "white planet" hovered serenely against the blue morning sky. What secrets was this daytime moon witnessing? Sidnei figured there would be some juicy things to report. Before moving on, she pulled her phone out of her pocket and snapped a quick picture of this daytime moon.

Sidnei began walking and welcomed the gentle September breeze. She took a deep breath and relished the earthy smells of the cornfields surrounding her. This was one of her favorite walks, ever changing, ever adapting. She loved everything about the approaching central-Pennsylvania fall. She watched the shorn cornstalks leisurely sway as she passed. Dotting the corn rows, late-summer weeds popped up defiantly. Field mice played hide-and-seek among the straggly rows. Sidnei bet those mice had their own secrets. She noticed the moon had taken cover behind a few clouds. Yes, Sidnei concluded, there was something of interest to the moon occurring on planet Earth. She smiled.

Having walked close to three miles through the cornfields, Sidnei felt the heat. Her curly blonde ponytail swung from side to side as she made her way toward her country home, absently batting at the gnats above her head. Her white jogging shorts and lightweight pink T-shirt now clung to her. Although she loved walking, Sidnei craved a shower, for she truly detested sweating. Stopping to stretch, Sidnei began to hum as she gazed once more at the dried cornstalks doing their dance. The moon had disappeared behind the clouds. She felt deeply alive as she took in big gulps of the late-summer air and contemplated the task before her.

It was the first Sunday of the month, the day to call her parents. She closed her eyes and replayed last month's conversation.

Her father had answered the phone with a tentative "Hello?"

"Hi, Dad! How are you?" asked Sidnei.

"Here—let me give the phone to your mother."

Her mother came right on the phone. "Sidnei, I've been so sick, nauseated, indigestion. And my knee hurts all the time."

Sidnei thought her mother sounded strangely breathless. "Have you seen the doctor?"

"Well, no, no ..."

"Maybe you should call and make an appointment."

"I better have you talk to your dad."

Sidnei heard the scratch of reception as the phone was passed between her parents. Then heavy breathing came across the phone.

"Dad, don't hang up."

"Okay, Sidnei. That's all for now." Then the phone went dead.

Sidnei had punched their number back in, but it had gone immediately to voice mail, which informed her it was full.

Sidnei opened her eyes, looked around, and realized she wasn't stretching anymore. She was no longer smiling either. A shiver ran through her body in spite of the heat. Those phone conversations preoccupied her thoughts more and more. There was a time when her phone conversations with her parents lasted for up to an hour. Her parents would fill her in on all the sporting and musical events they had attended. While Sidnei had never been much interested in the information, she had to admit that they had at least had conversations in the past. Over the last few years, the calls had become increasingly brief and generally ended in her parents abruptly ending the call. What was up with that? she asked herself.

Shading her eyes from the sun, she looked in the direction of her home. Logan, her husband, was hunkered over their post-mounted mailbox and newspaper holder. She had designed the mount, and he had built it. They were so proud of their teamwork on this project when they first moved into their country home. She was pretty sure he was reading the newspaper now. It was one of the first things he did each morning. She felt a familiar rush of love as she looked him over. His tousled brown curls fell over his forehead. He bit his lower lip. Those two things always got her.

Sidnei began walking again, picking up her pace as she got closer to Logan. She called his name, and Logan looked up. A broad smile took over Logan's tanned face. His six-foot frame slowly straightened.

"Hey! How is it out there today?" Logan asked as Sidnei reached him.

"Hot—very, very, very hot! And buggy. There are bugs flying around my head and bugs inside my head."

Logan laughed and folded up the paper.

"I'm betting you want to talk about today's phone call," said Logan.

"Yes. I need you to brainstorm the situation with me. It's starting to worry me a little."

Together, they moved toward the garage.

"Okay. I'm here," he said.

Sidnei sat on the second step leading to the garage, unlacing her shoes.

"When I do reach them, their end of the conversation is always the same. They have ailments but don't see the doctor. They pass the phone back and forth like it's a hot potato. Then they end the call without any warning. I'm stymied."

She peered up at Logan and continued. "Should I have the police visit them? I know that sounds drastic, but …"

"That'll set your dad off. He wouldn't understand why you sent them. It would just make him angry."

"Okay. I know you're right. So how about if I asked one of their neighbors to look in on them?"

"That sounds like another misunderstood intervention. They probably wouldn't even answer the door. And that neighborhood is full of transients."

Sidnei sat up straight, focusing fully on Logan.

"How about visiting them in Phoenix ourselves?" he said.

Sidnei shook her head. "No. I don't want to … yet I feel like I should. But I have that photo assignment in Iceland coming up. I don't know what to do. Damn!" Sidnei swiped at a tear rolling down her face.

Logan sat beside her on the steps. "I know. They've never made it easy for you." He took her hand in his.

They sat in silence for a few moments until Sidnei got up.

"I need a good shower to help cleanse and organize my thoughts. I'll be back soon." She wiped her lingering tears away, hunched her shoulders, and slowly moved into the house, humming a single note to help focus her thoughts as she made her way to the master bedroom suite.

Her bedroom was a cozy, comfortable haven. Antiques and artwork collected on her travels decorated the sunlit room. The quilt she and Logan had designed together covered the queen-size bed. They had searched for just the right pieces to complete the wagon-wheel design in shades of blue, cranberry, and forest green. She shrugged out of her walking clothes and entered a steamy, warm shower.

Sidnei emerged in the kitchen thirty minutes later. She now boasted a french braid. Her tanned skin glistened beneath her sheer pink robe. The whole room was filled with the faint scent of roses from her lotion.

Sidnei sauntered over to the espresso machine. After preparing a double espresso, she blew a kiss to Logan, who was seated at the kitchen table, as she made her way to the sun porch, actually her writing studio. The view from this room always soothed her. A field line defined the border of their back property. It was filled with oak trees, sumac, wildflowers, and wild berry bushes. Crows and songbirds floated in and out of the trees. Maples, honey locusts, lindens, and hawthorns peppered the landscape coming up to the house. Sidnei took great pride in knowing she had planted all these trees herself. A family of hummingbirds flitted from hummingbird feeder to hummingbird feeder. Sidnei liked to think of all this as her own private magic show. Life popped up all around her, and she had only to enjoy it. With the breeze today, her trees moved in a free-form jig. A calm settled over her as she felt herself centering in this space. She was ready to look at the issue—or at least begin to spell it out more clearly. She took a deep breath and returned to the kitchen and Logan.

"Okay, Logan, I'll get dressed. Ready to go to lunch in about fifteen minutes?"

"Sounds good."

Sidnei returned to her bedroom and entered her walk-in closet. Different shades of the color spectrum surrounded her. There were dresses, skirts, blouses, pants, jeans, tunics, and accessories galore. And the shoes! Well, Sidnei loved shoes. They took up a whole wall of the closet. For today, she pictured herself in something that moved like the breeze. She tried a few color combinations with dresses and shawls. When she was satisfied with her choices, Sidnei came out strutting in a guava-colored dress that skimmed her knees. A peach shawl shimmied on her hips. Pale pink flats completed the ensemble. Pink diamonds sparkled in her ears. She thought she looked a little like the sunset.

Sidnei twirled as she came into the kitchen. "I'm ready for anything at the moment."

"Then let's go!"

A short drive brought the two of them to their favorite restaurant, Chez Arlette. It was dressed up with French country antiques and Provencal linens. Sidnei and Logan were seated at a table by the window overlooking the fall-colored hills. Leaves of gold, yellow, and red floated to the ground outside. Quiet conversations and the clink of cutlery and crystal glasses filled the dining room. They ordered a bottle of wine and settled into their well-cushioned chairs.

Sidnei carefully studied Logan for a few moments before she began to speak. They were a team, and she knew that together they could make sense out of the growing puzzle of her parents.

"So, I'm going to jump right in." Sidnei slowly set her wineglass down. "I don't understand why my parents can't answer the phone. When I was growing up, my parents always seemed to be busy doing something. Now, I have a sense that they aren't busy at all. I don't think they even go to church anymore. I never hear about sporting events or jazz concerts. You know, come to think of it, I don't hear about their friends anymore either."

"Have they mentioned Garvan or his kids lately?" Logan asked.

"You know, they haven't. That's odd." Sidnei ran her fingers up and down the stem of her wineglass.

"Your parents have always been a little—I don't know—secretive, maybe preoccupied."

"I've thought they were elusive in the past. But now they're decidedly guarded. Oh, I don't know …" Sidnei stared into her wineglass. "Like they're hiding something." Her fingers tapped the table as the image of the moon earlier filled her head. She caught herself gasping a little and felt an old familiar scraping of her heart.

"Sid?"

"Oh, sorry. I was just thinking." Sidnei took a sip of wine and focused her attention on Logan. "Let me go back a few years."

"Okay, but if you're going where I think you're going, it may be a little rough."

"No, I'm good. I need to make some sense out of our last visit three years ago."

"I'm listening." Logan leaned forward.

"All right. Here are the facts. We made our annual trip to Phoenix. Mom was her usual shadowy self, but Dad was agitated, jumpy, pacing around their family room, almost like he was on cocaine or something. We had picked up a bouquet of red roses for Mom that Dad grabbed out of my hands. He then held it over my head threateningly and told me loudly I needed to bring Mom something she could use, like money."

"That's when I got worried and moved you quickly out of his way."

"And out the door. My heart still races when I think about that incident. He had hollered at me my whole life but never like that." Sidnei sat back in her chair.

Their chateaubriand arrived. The conversation stopped while dazzling servings of prime beef and fresh vegetables were artistically ladled onto individual plates. They thanked the waiter, who moved away.

"You know, they've never made things easy for you."

"But why money? I know we've talked about this before, but asking for money made no sense. They've always seemed to be comfortable."

Sidnei closed her eyes for a moment. She envisioned the family room at her parents' house. It was decorated in red, white, and blue with collectibles and comfy colonial furniture. She opened her eyes and seemed to see the food she had been served for the first time. They ate in silence for a few minutes.

"I still think we should go down there. You seem to have more and more questions that we can't answer."

"I just don't know. That last visit was so strange." Sidnei moved the food around on her plate. She looked up at Logan and then took a breath. "Let's enjoy our meal for now and continue this conversation at home." She smiled, and they finished their meal quietly.

Once home, Logan poured each one of them a cognac. They walked together to the living room where original landscapes adorned the walls and complemented the fall scene outside the expansive picture window.

"I love this room," said Sidnei. She looked around the room and then snuggled into an oversize armchair with a gold-and-lavender leaf pattern.

"I was thinking about this whole situation on the way home." Logan sat in a similar chair.

"Me too. In fact, I can't stop thinking about it. I chose to keep in touch. They're my parents, after all. Somehow, though, they seem almost unreachable." Sidnei inhaled the scent of the cognac and closed her eyes.

"I have to ask—even though I know you don't want me to. Your other two brothers, Aiden and Tam, why did they stop communicating with your parents?"

Sidnei slowly opened her eyes. "That was ages ago, and I honestly don't know. You know my family. They don't talk much."

"Do you know how to contact either one of them?"

"No, no. I wouldn't know where to start. I was never too crazy about any of the three of my brothers. You know that. Garvan, in particular, sucked the life out of my mother. Where are you going with this?" Sidnei asked.

"I was thinking they might have some clues. That's all." Logan shrugged.

They both sipped their cognacs.

"I might add that they had very little to do with me as we grew up, other than my giving them rides to practices and babysitting them sometimes. You might recall my status in the family."

"Yes, I do."

"Garvan is the only one of them that's kept up with Mom and Dad. I think he actually lives with them sometimes, although neither Mom nor Dad would confirm that. I do know he drifts from job to job, so he probably depends upon them more than he should. It's kind of sad since he's fifty years old." Sidnei's voice grew quieter. Her gaze was distant.

"I always found him creepy, always lurking around," Logan said.

"Creepy. Needy. How about shiftless?" Sidnei looked over at Logan.

"I think we need to know where he is now."

Sidnei could feel her heart pulsing, her breath slowing. "Okay, Logan. I'm going to make the call."

They both waited expectantly, but on the tenth ring, it went to voice mail. Sidnei ended the call. "Damn!"

"So what do you want to do?"

"I want more time to think about it. And I want a hug." She got up, went over to Logan, and settled in his lap with her arms wrapped around his neck. He hugged her tightly. They sat there until the nearly full moon came up and illuminated the night.

2

Four-year-old Sidnei woke up sluggishly as her body rocked with the train. She rubbed her eyes and then looked up at the moon. The moon cast an otherworldly glow over the sleeping car. Sidnei shook her rumpled blonde curls, catching the glint of the moon on those curls.

"Ohhh …" she quietly squealed as she caught her reflection in the window.

Bringing the soft squeal down to a whisper, Sidnei said, "It's your magic, Moon. You put magic in my hair."

"Shhh, Sidnei. You'll wake your brother," said her daddy from the opposite berth.

Sidnei looked to her right, taking in the sleeping bulk that was Aiden. He had curly red hair, and freckles covered his body from head to toe. Two-year-old Aiden wasn't much of a playmate for her, more a nuisance taking up her parents' time and attention. He hardly even talked. He smelled sometimes. He cried a lot of the time. He sucked his thumb when he slept, like right now.

Sidnei glanced toward the other berth and responded in a whisper, "Oh, Daddy, he's very, very sound asleep."

"Okay, Sidnei, but let's be quiet."

"Daddy, the moon is like in a fairy tale."

"Sure, Sidnei. Just don't wake Aiden."

Sidnei knew her daddy could not see her, but she nodded anyway. Still staring at the night sky, she wondered if there were little children like her on the moon, looking down at her train. Maybe they were sending her messages in the sparkles glancing off the train windows. She continued to take in the brilliance of the full moon until the train's motion lulled her back to sleep. Her dreams were filled with games of hide-and-seek with the children on the moon.

Morning brought harsh sunlight and hurried preparations for the day. Sidnei was told to dress quickly in her red velvet dress while her mommy brushed out her curls and braided them into two tight, stiff plaits. Her daddy dressed Aiden while he squirmed and whined. Suitcases were snapped shut.

Sidnei carefully looked over her family members. They were all dressed for church. Her mommy had on a beige suit with a coordinating cap sleeve pullover, and she wore a hat with feathers like the new Queen Elizabeth. Her golden-hued hair was pulled back in a bun. Her daddy wore a corduroy sport coat and trousers. His own tight curls were still a little damp. Aiden had on a sweater and slacks and even a tie. Sidnei wondered what place they might visit. She really hoped it wasn't church.

"Ready, guys?" asked her daddy. He looked his family over carefully, playfully yanked one of Sidnei's braids, and then marched the four of them off the train. Her daddy took Aiden's hand. Her mommy reached for Sidnei's hand.

Her daddy led them toward a car, which he pointed to in the distance. A tall, lanky, older man stood by the car waving at them. The car was a station wagon, blue in the front, yellow on the sides, and brown wood on the back end. It looked very, very big to Sidnei.

As Sidnei walked beside her parents, she peered up at her daddy. He had that glint in his eye that she could never quite figure out. It made her daddy's eyes all murky like ice cubes. She thought it best for now to just look around her.

Moving slowly through the burgeoning crowd, Sidnei took in her new surroundings. The air was filled with the screech of trains pulling up on tracks. Fumes of grease and diesel competed for her senses. Tumbles of steam whirled from a different track where the engines had round faces. Sidnei looked in both directions, a little confused by the different engines. The engine of the train in which she had traveled was sleek, with a round, smallish mouth on its face. All about her, both people and machines darted. The people swarmed around her from every direction. People wearing matching outfits pushed around carts filled with suitcases. As the people swirled around her, they waved and shouted hello to other people. Sidnei thought this must be what people called commotion.

Many of the people were dressed differently here. Some of them wore cowboy hats and cowboy boots. A couple of grown-up men had on bib overalls like Aiden wore sometimes.

"Where are we, Mommy?" asked Sidnei.

Without looking at Sidnei, her mommy replied blandly, "Denver. We've made it to Denver." She clasped Sidnei's hand more tightly.

"Are those real cowboys?" asked Sidnei.

"Shhhh, Sidnei. Behave, please," said her mommy, still looking off into the distance.

"But, Mommy …"

"This is to be a new beginning, Sidnei. You'll see," said her mommy. Her mommy looked toward her daddy as she said this.

"Okay, but will I see my friends?"

"You'll make new friends." Her mommy's grip tightened on Sidnei's hand.

"Yes, but will they like me?" Sidnei was twisting her hand to try to loosen her mommy's grip.

"Oh, Sidnei, everyone loves you." Her mommy let go of her hand.

They were almost to the tall man. Her daddy motioned for the three of them to form a line behind him as they drew closer to the man who kept waving at them. Close up, the station wagon was even larger than Sidnei had thought. Beside it was a pickup truck that was dwarfed by the large station wagon. Sidnei giggled softly. Her daddy looked at her sternly.

As the young family approached, the man asked, "Coach Gabe Jepson?"

"Yes, sir!" said her daddy. With a wide smile, her daddy introduced his family. "This is Jezzi, my wife, Aiden, my son, and Sidnei, my daughter." All shook hands.

When her daddy got to Sidnei, the tall man smiled and said, "My! Aren't you a pretty little thing!"

"Thank you, but I'm not little. I'm a big girl," said Sidnei, looking straight up at the man.

"Well, yes. Yes. I can see that, young lady," said the man, winking at her daddy.

"Sidnei, just say thank you," said her daddy as he directed Sidnei and Aiden to the back seat of the car.

"Thank you, sir," said Sidnei from inside the car.

Her daddy and the tall man said a few more things to each other, exchanged envelopes, and shook hands before her daddy climbed into the driver's seat. He smiled at her mommy and then twisted around to look at Sidnei.

"Sidnei, you are a big girl, so you know to be polite." He winked at her.

"Yes, Daddy," she said. Sidnei looked straight ahead, a little pout forming on her face.

"Thanks for meeting us!" her daddy hollered as he pulled the station wagon away from the curb. He carefully maneuvered the car into the traffic.

"Gabe?" asked her mommy.

"It's part of the deal. This is going to be good. You'll all see," her daddy said. "Look, it has one of those new car radios. Let me just search for a jazz tune."

Her mommy looked on as her daddy kept one hand on the steering wheel while with the other hand he used the radio button to search for music. Single gulps of words from songs were caught until he found one he liked. The Tony guy her mommy and daddy liked was now warbling away about riches, right inside their car.

Sidnei sat back in her seat, taking in the continuing bustle outside the car. Cars instead of people now moved around them. Aiden had already fallen asleep. A little drool formed on the corner of his mouth. Already asleep even though so much was happening. *Aiden the dumb-dumb,* she thought.

Sidnei looked back to see the train station looming in the distance. As she turned in her seat, cars zoomed by on either side of her. There were lots of blue ones and red ones, and her eyes widened when she spied a couple the color of canned peas. They almost all had two big eyeballs in the front for lights. There were lots and lots of big buildings right next to one another. Her daddy slowed down when he neared what he called the Civic Center park area. It didn't really look like a park to Sidnei. There was a huge crowd of people there, which her daddy called extras for a movie about someone named Glenn Miller. How could people be extras? Sidnei wondered. Was that like second helpings? Her attention was drawn to a huge movie marquee announcing the movie *Peter Pan.* Boy would she like to see that! Sidnei looked at her parents.

"Where are we going?" she asked.

"Your new home," said her daddy. "You're going to love it!"

"Like my new friends will love me," said Sidnei.

"That's my girl! Gonna have your own room too!"

"Gabe, a house? With more than two bedrooms?" asked her mommy.

"That's right! Nothing too good for my family!"

While her daddy moved his new car in and out of the traffic, Sidnei noticed her mommy had become silent.

"Are you missing your friends too, Mommy?" Sidnei asked.

Her mommy quietly said, "Yes."

"Now, girls, you're both gonna love this place!" said her daddy.

Sidnei didn't really think you could feel silence, but everyone had grown so quiet. No one was speaking, but it sure felt like someone or something else was here waiting to be addressed. The air around Sidnei felt different somehow. Looking up at the sky, Sidnei saw only clouds. She decided she should be quiet for a while. But gosh! She still had a lot of questions left. She squeezed her eyes shut and quickly fell asleep, thinking about what the moon children might be doing right now.

3

Sidnei woke on Monday to the music of rain. She held her eyes shut and pretended she was behind a waterfall in her happy place. She wondered why her parents never appeared in these journeys. Logan often did. For a few moments, she continued to listen to the patter of the waterfall and the rain, suspended in that place between sleeping and waking.

Slowly, Sidnei opened her eyes. It was a new day. Maybe her parents would answer their phone today. Logan was up and gone to work, she knew. Sidnei eased into her day with a double expresso, followed by a quick jaunt through her neighborhood. Each home was built on one to two acres, giving the neighborhood a feeling of openness. Fences were not allowed, so dogs stood behind invisible fencing, barking half-hearted warnings as Sidnei jogged by. In the distance, someone walked their dog on a leash. Several neighbors waved to her as she passed. Sidnei smiled and waved back.

The air was still today, but her thoughts were not. Sidnei was familiar with her feelings and knew she was in denial. She also knew denial was destined to move toward anger. She had to get a grip on this. She had not seen her parents for a few years, but things could change. Logan was right. She needed to see them to get over her doubts concerning their health issues, as well as the pictures forming in her mind regarding their self-enforced isolation. She liked knowing almost all was right in her world. As she continued to jog, looking right and left, Sidnei could tick off what was right and good about each resident, each home, each planting, each turn in the road.

Sweat trickled down Sidnei's spine as she came in view of her home. She had been totally unaware that she was moving at such a rapid pace. Stopping, she stretched and looked around her. Her home was a low, broad 5,400-square-foot Cape Cod with a steep pitched gabled roof, a large central chimney, and symmetrically located windows with a central front door. She loved how the symmetry and simplicity contrasted with the expansive English cottage garden that rolled down to the street. Sidnei found something spontaneous about the beauty of it all. Late-summer pollinators and monarch butterflies gracefully fed in her lush front garden.

She finished her stretches and moved into the day. Her preparations were minimal, as she planned to stay close to home today. There were flights to look into, which had to work around her trip to Iceland, more notes to gather about Iceland and the northern lights, vegetables aplenty to harvest from the side garden, and the phone call to be attempted. First, she chose to work in the garden.

Sidnei could recite her parents' litanies of health complaints they offered each month. The ailments were always the same—knees, mobility, faulty eyesight, memory. Actual doctor visits to address these issues were rare. Sidnei did not know if the ailments were real. When she last visited her parents, they were perfectly fine, hardy even. They had always been active. She supposed something could have happened, but they never mentioned anything.

Sidnei picked the last ripe vegetable and looked over her harvest for the morning. There were lusciously plump bell peppers, layers of tomatoes, carrots, onions, and a delicata squash. A head of garlic crowned the bounty. Sidnei took the vegetables inside and washed and stored them. Her thoughts moved into questions. If Garvan was living with them, why wasn't he making sure they saw a doctor when they needed to? Why wasn't Garvan insisting they get out more? It was, after all, his girls who played in all those ball games her parents had attended. Come to think of it, those girls had not been mentioned in the phone calls in quite some time. Why not? And why didn't Garvan ever answer the phone? Anger seeped in. Sidnei sighed.

Her phone began to ring. Picking it up, Sidnei noticed the number had a 602 area code—Phoenix. Her heart began thumping. Her head pounded. Sidnei answered, "Yes? Hello?"

"Hello! I'm Zelly McNulty. I'm a nurse for Desert Senior Health Services and the case manager for your parents. I'm here talking to them, and they mentioned that they hadn't heard from you in a while."

"Well, no. I do try to call once a month. You're *there*? How often do you see them?"

"Ah, yes. Yes. I've actually checked on your parents for a few years now. For the past year, I've been stopping by to see them about once a week."

"Once a week? Should I be alarmed that you're making home visits?" Sidnei made her way to the nearest chair.

"Oh no. Home visits are common with the elderly, especially when they're homebound. Let me just move to the next room."

Sidnei heard a door close before Zelly returned to talk. "As I was saying—"

Sidnei quickly cut in, "Homebound?"

"Sidnei, I don't want to alarm you, but it's been necessary for me to come more frequently this past year. Your dad's macular degeneration and your mom's dementia are taking a toll, a pretty hefty toll at that."

"Zelly, right? I haven't seen my parents in years. I have no idea what you're talking about. The last time I saw them, they were planning a trip to a jazz festival in Sacramento and going to their granddaughters' softball games several times a week." Sidnei had been pacing. She stopped and took a deep breath.

"I think you need to come see for yourself. They currently have no doctor, which I prefer to discuss with you in person," said Zelly.

"Well, I ... I have to think about all this. Frankly, I'm not so sure they really want to see me."

There was a short silence on the other end of the line. Sidnei could hear Zelly clearing her throat.

"Sidnei, I know this is probably a lot for you to take in, but I believe you need to see the situation in person. I'm worried. I like your parents. I would like to meet with you. I will tell you that the house has become pretty cluttered."

Sidnei knew *that* could not be true. Her mother always kept her home clean and tidy—obsessively so. Never was anything out of place. Never!

"That's just not possible. My mom's always been an impeccable housekeeper," said Sidnei, fear in her voice.

"Sidnei, I want to prepare you for what I'm seeing," said Zelly.

"Of course. I need time to think though ... I'll see what I can do."

"Thank you," said Zelly. "Do you want to talk to your mom or dad?"

"Do they want to speak with me?"

There was muffled conversation. Doors opened and closed. Then Zelly came back on. "They say they're good. I really hope we can meet soon. You can reach me through Desert Senior Health Services. Goodbye for now."

"And I can be reached at this number. Goodbye," said Sidnei. Her thoughts raced. *No? They were good for now?* But of course they didn't want to talk to her. They would have to wiggle around questions. The king and queen of evasion might be ill, but they were still operating in escape mode.

Sidnei could feel her heart beating but felt nothing down deep inside, not even an achiness. She simply stood with her phone in her hand for several minutes. Then she moved to her computer and researched flights to Phoenix. She would have to work around her photo assignment, but that appeared to be doable. The distraction was helping, but oh how she wanted to cry, to scream—but about what? And at whom? She sat for long minutes in front of her computer and stared.

As evening approached, Sidnei pulled herself into the kitchen. She opened the refrigerator to take stock of what she had on hand for dinner. The kitchen was soon sizzling with spicy fragrances. Hearing Logan's car pull into the garage, Sidnei poured a couple of glasses of wine, set them on the counter, and waited.

When Logan entered the kitchen, he took just one quick look at Sidnei before asking, "You connected today, didn't you?"

Sidnei's eyes filled with tears. That blank spot in her heart began to fill.

"Yes … no. Not with them exactly. My parents are ill and stuck at home. They don't even have a doctor."

"How do you know?" He moved toward Sidnei and put his hands on her shoulders.

"They have a case manager who was visiting them today, a nurse. She was assigned to them from their health care plan. She didn't want to share too much until she could meet with me in person. She says I need to see how things are. It doesn't sound good." Sidnei hung her head and leaned into Logan's chest.

"We've both been thinking things weren't right. Let's go, Sidnei. Let's just pick up and go." He gently kissed the top of her head. "Let's just go."

"I did look up flights," said Sidnei in a whisper.

"Good. Let's look at them together. Sounds like we need to go as soon as we can."

"Uh-huh," said Sidnei quietly.

"Did this person mention Garvan?" asked Logan.

Sidnei looked up at Logan. "No, no she didn't. That's odd," said Sidnei, her voice trailing off.

Sidnei felt an old, unnerving dread growing. She accepted a glass of wine from Logan and headed outside. As she began to walk among her trees and gardens, the moon appeared on the horizon, washed in a bloodred haze. Sidnei shivered. She leaned against a tree and started to sob. Slowly she slid down to the ground and pulled her arms across her chest, barricading her heart while still clutching her wineglass. The moon continued to rise with scarlet rivulets snaking across it.

4

Squeezing her Babee Bee doll tightly, Sidnei looked around her pink-and-purple bedroom. Boxes, lots and lots of boxes, had almost all her things in them. Only her doll's carrying case and her Mickey Mouse phonograph remained unpacked. Her canopy bed frame had even been taken down and packed. Her bed rested naked in the middle of the room, no dust ruffle, no sheets, no bedspread, just bare.

"Ready to go, Sidnei?" asked her dad. He filled the doorway to her bedroom.

"Sure, Dad, but why are we moving again?"

"Opportunity, Sidnei, opportunity. You'll see. New school. New friends. You'll see." Her dad followed his answer with a wink.

"Friends are hard when we keep moving," said Sidnei. She was trying not to pout, but it was hard. Sidnei looked carefully at her dad. He wore a grin and carried a basketball, just like always. She guessed she could try to smile.

"Sidnei, you have to be the one who introduces yourself. You're pretty and smart. You'll see. You'll make new friends."

"Okay, Dad! I guess I'm ready then." She hugged her doll as her smile slowly began to falter. Her shoulders fell as she walked through her bedroom door. The pink-and-purple bedroom would soon belong to another little girl.

Sidnei walked ahead of her dad. He followed, moving the basketball from hand to hand as he whistled.

When the two of them walked out the front door, Aiden and Tam,

Sidnei's two brothers, came running up. Aiden had grown really tall. Tam was darker, stockier. Immediately, her dad passed the ball to Aiden, who, in turn, passed it on to Tam. This continued while Sidnei stood by and watched. She always watched. She watched her dad's teams play. She watched Aiden play. She watched Tam play. Her mom said Sidnei could be a cheerleader. Sidnei knew that meant she could watch even more games. The cheerleaders at her dad's team games were always acting goofy around him. Ugh! What Sidnei really wanted to do was to check out the astronomy club at her new school. Her mom didn't think that was such a good idea, which meant her dad really, really didn't think it was a good idea. Sidnei was often told that she didn't have good ideas. When she went to bed at night, though, she came up with all kinds of good ideas in the dark. Sidnei smiled now as she watched the basketball pass from one boy to another.

She giggled when she realized she had thought of her dad as a boy. He was always kind of acting like one, sort of like Peter Pan. He didn't seem to want to grow up. Her dad moved her family around a lot, and Peter Pan did flit from one place to another. The similarity ended there though. After all, Sidnei wasn't included in the boys' games. Neither was her mom. The two of them either watched the boys or stayed at home.

But one day, someday, Sidnei was going to do something they would all come and watch together. The thought made her feel like flying, or dancing, or singing. These kinds of things always made her smile. She spun into a pirouette and began to sing.

"Sidnei, for land's sakes, stop that! You're distracting us!" Her dad had a mean look on his face.

"Sorry, Dad," said Sidnei as she slunk away. She stopped on the opposite side of the house to watch the movers carry boxes to the moving van. She blinked a few times to keep the tears away and then silently reentered her thoughts. Sidnei looked around quickly to make sure no one was paying any attention to her. Whew! Good! She imagined each box held a secret and magical idea like each of her ideas at night. One day, one of those ideas would pop out and set her free, free to be Sidnei.

Her mom was walking toward her. She often wondered what her mom did all day while she was at school. Her friends' mothers all worked. One was even a policewoman. Her mom was always cleaning house—always. Of course, her mom did go to lots of ball games, but so did the other moms. Humph!

"Hi, Mom!"

"Shhh, Sidnei! It's not ladylike to shout. It's about time to go. Are all your things ready?"

"Sure, Mom," said Sidnei. She held Babee Bee with one hand.

She stood alongside her mom and took one last look at their latest home. It had been a pretty good one, she guessed. It was, after all, their first real house. Her dad had not only taught and coached, but he also worked to help young adults transition from drug rehabilitation facilities to jobs in the community. Lots of people liked him for that. She wondered why they couldn't stay. But then they never seemed to stay long anywhere. Her dad just hopped from one school job to another. People would come to the house with a young lady who cried a lot, and then boom, they were moving. Shrugging, Sidnei reached for her mom's hand, and together they walked to the car.

"We'll try to have your bed put together by tomorrow evening. Tonight, we'll all sleep in sleeping bags at the new house. It'll be like camping out. Won't this be fun?" Her mom sounded a little breathless and looked blankly ahead.

"Just like Peter Pan!" said Sidnei. She smiled down at her doll.

"Well, yes! What fun!" said her mom. She too was smiling a wee little smile.

"Well, well, well! Here are my two happy girls! Ready to go?" asked her dad.

"Sure," said her mom. Sidnei studied her mom for a minute. She didn't think her mom was really ready.

The family clambered into the car. Her dad stopped by the curb for one final look, and then they were off. Sidnei sat in the back seat with her two brothers. The two boys squirmed and fussed with each other. They left Sidnei alone. She had proven long ago that she was a formidable foe who would not be dallied with. Sidnei thought they were jerks and didn't want to be bothered. Aiden and Tam knew the score.

Sidnei now had time to generate ideas, to herself of course. Her dad had said they would paint her new bedroom any color she liked. This would take some doing, as she was thinking sky-blue walls with the stars and moon and planets on the ceiling. Her dad would put his basketball down when she told him this. She needed a plan.

Sidnei reached for her bag and drew out her tablet and a pencil. She searched the tablet for her drawing of the planets. She had all the planets strategically revolving around the sun. The moon was peeking out from behind some fluffy clouds. Sidnei smiled. It would be an amazing ceiling. Now if her dad would just let her do it this way. *C'mon, my old pal Moon and the moon children too*, she thought, *let this happen for me.* Sidnei squeezed her eyes shut and crossed her fingers on each hand.

It wasn't long before her dad announced they had arrived at their new home across town. The announcement jarred Sidnei out of her reverie. She stared. The house was two stories and had white brick walls. There was a huge yard surrounding it. Wow!

Sidnei slid out of the back seat. When she stood on the sidewalk, she quickly spied three girls about her age looking at her from across the street. She stared back.

"Well, well, well, Sidnei. Ready-made friends just waiting for you!" said her dad.

"Dad, I don't even know their names."

"You will, Sidnei, you will."

"Sidnei, let's get inside and get ready for our campout," said her mom, a worried frown on her face.

"Coming, Mom." Sidnei glanced at the girls across the street one more time. Slowly she made her way through the front door. Steps leading upstairs met her just inside the door. The rooms were big and empty.

As the evening unfolded, Sidnei was not impressed by the adventure. The new house was big but very, very white in every room. There were no curtains. The boxes would not arrive until tomorrow. The sleeping bags remained stacked in the corner of the living room. Her dad and brothers went out to get dinner and returned with—yuck!—hot dogs. She hated them! The ruddy cylinders filled the buns and were covered with a wad of stinky sauerkraut.

Sidnei prepared to get yelled at for not finishing her dinner. She picked bites of her bun from the edges. Swallowing a gulp of milk, she looked to the right and to the left to gauge who might be watching her. No one yet. Maybe she could ditch the gross thing, but where? Sidnei carefully replaced the offending dog in its wrapper. She quietly asked if she could finish eating outside so she could explore the yard a little. Her parents merely nodded her way as they continued their discussion about where the furniture should be put, especially the new black-and-white TV. Jazz played softly from the old striped radio beside them.

Sidnei slipped out the front door and moved around to the back of the house. The yard was nice; big trees and bushes with flowers dotted the landscape. The previous residents had left a swing set. As Sidnei glided in one of the swings, she slowly picked the hot dog to pieces, which she then crushed into the wrapper. Finding garbage cans beside the garage, she deposited the remains with a giggle. This was too easy! She returned inside, asked for another glass of milk, and went back outside to sit on the back porch and watch the stars come out.

The moon was only a sliver, but she bet she could still hide behind it. What else could she hide behind? A mountain, a tree, a waterfall ... With a waterfall, she could stand behind it and watch others walk by. Cool! Sidnei closed her eyes and imagined what that would be like. Her face filled with a smile. This was her kind of place she was imagining. No one could bother her. No brothers could find her.

In the background, she heard her name being called. Sidnei opened one eye and saw a bright star peering down at her. She was going to check on that astronomy club. She was! She stood up.

"I'm here, Mom," said Sidnei.

"Good! We're ready to roll out the sleeping bags."

"I hope I can read for a while."

"Sure you can. Your dad brought flashlights," said her mom, with one of what Sidnei identified as her mom's fake smiles.

Teeth brushed, pajamas on, brothers settled, finally Sidnei could read. She soon discovered that even with an air mattress under the sleeping bag, her bed for the night was not very comfortable. Sitting up, she read into the night with her flashlight. When she did crawl into her sleeping bag, she closed her eyes and was once again transported behind the waterfall. She imagined layers and layers of soft leaves underneath her, safe and comfortable. Sleep came easily.

The boxes were already arriving when Sidnei awoke. Her mom hurried her into the bathroom to get ready for the day. Sidnei would be enrolling in her new school this morning. She brushed her blonde curls until they shined. Smoothing her new plaid dress and standing on her tiptoes in her brand-spanking-new saddle shoes, she smiled into the mirror.

"Mom, I'm ready!"

"Okay, Sidnei! Aiden's almost ready too."

"I'll wait outside," said Sidnei. She sailed out the front door.

Sidnei watched the movers manipulate the bigger boxes from the moving van. She saw her name on a few of these boxes. It was a little like Christmas, she thought, because she didn't know what was in each box, but she knew what she was expecting. Actually, this was even better because she was guaranteed what she expected. Sidnei saw her mom coming around from the garage.

"Time to go, Sidnei."

"Coming, Mom."

Sidnei took one more look at the movers. Her dad and Tam watched them too, she noticed. As each box came off the truck, her dad told the movers which room it would need to go to. Sidnei waved goodbye. Her dad waved back with one hand while twirling the basketball on one finger of the other hand. A couple of the movers waved to her too. Once she saw the stereo cabinet unloaded, Sidnei skipped over to the car, which her mom had pulled out of the garage. Sidnei stopped just a moment to ask that first-day-at-a-new-school-knot-in-her-stomach to please go away. She wanted to have fun today.

As she settled into the back seat, Sidnei asked, "Mom, why do we have to move so often?"

"Sidnei, don't ask so many questions! You'll love your new school! You'll love your new friends! Now, let's get ready for a good day!"

Her mom's jaw was set, and her face expressionless. Sidnei knew that meant she should be quiet. Today she just couldn't.

"Mom, new schools and new friends are hard. The kids always stare at me. I have to eat by myself for a long, long time. It's hard, Mom, not fun," said Sidnei.

"Now, Sidnei, remember what your favorite thing about school is." The irritation in her mom's voice was growing apparent. She turned the radio off.

"Mom, you know it's learning. And I want to learn more about space!" Sidnei crossed her arms over her chest.

That strange silence took over the car. Sidnei had been imagining lately that it had arms and legs and was covered with hair, lots of it, enough to smother a person. Aiden stared at her from the other side of the back seat. Sidnei looked out the window. Well, why couldn't anyone answer her question with a real reason? Other kids didn't have to move. Other kids had the same friends forever. As her mom pulled into the parking lot of the new school, Sidnei blinked away her tears. The three girls from last night stood in front of the school and stared as Sidnei's mom parked the car.

5

As the plane made its descent toward Phoenix, Sidnei looked out at the brown landscape dotted with brush. There was dust, and dirt, and sand, all dreary as a crumpled brown paper bag. To be sure, the saguaro cacti stood tall and majestic, but Sidnei knew from long hikes in this desert that even they often had broken appendages.

Sidnei reached over and took Logan's hand. She squeezed it, and he squeezed back as he kissed the top of her head.

"We'll make it fine, whatever it is," said Logan.

"I know, but Zelly has me really freaked out. When I spoke to her about this visit, she reiterated that the house was pretty cluttered. When I talked to Mom to tell her we were coming to visit, Mom sounded pretty spacey."

"C'mon, there isn't much of anything we haven't been able to sort out together over the years."

Looking at each other as the plane touched down, they squeezed hands.

"Ready?" Logan said.

"As ready as I'm ever going to be," Sidnei said.

They gathered their carry-ons and made their way to the designated baggage carousel. Looking around while waiting for their bags, Sidnei couldn't help but notice that almost everyone appeared older, much older, than she and Logan were. Everyone had on shorts and tank tops, flip-flops or sturdy sandals, not things her parents would be inclined to wear. Most were actively engaged with their cell phones, something Sidnei could not imagine either of her parents doing.

"Here come the bags already. I'll just grab them," said Logan.

Their bags were hot pink with bright purple identification tags. They were intended for fun trips like hers to Iceland, thought Sidnei, as opposed to the unknowns awaiting them, no doubt, on this trip. A sigh burst from Sidnei. Logan shot her a reassuring smile.

Sidnei and Logan exited the terminal and were blinded by the sun. It was unforgivably hot. The sun actually prickled Sidnei's exposed skin. They hustled to the waiting area for rental car patrons.

"Not much relief under here," said Logan.

"You know, my dad flew from Seattle to here for years." Sidnei continued with her visual inspection as the heat broiled up from the asphalt.

"I would have to *really* want to be here in this heat versus Seattle."

"Me too! I never understood why they chose Phoenix as their final destination. They moved so often, and there were so many places with milder climates that they could have returned to," said Sidnei.

"There's also the mystery of that neighborhood they live in. They lived in some pretty cool places over the years since I've known them—like Seattle. And how about the country club place? Cherry Hills in Colorado, I think it was. Their place in Walnut Creek in California was pretty nice too."

"You're right. They were pretty cool."

"Here comes the shuttle. Let's get the rental car and begin this, this … I don't know. Let's just keep moving," said Logan.

Sidnei considered Logan for a few moments as the shuttle meandered along its way to the rental car center. His parents had passed away rather suddenly when a drunk driver drove head-on into their car shortly after she and Logan had married. That was only months after they had graduated from high school. Logan was always very respectful of her parents, but they certainly had not always been respectful of him. She feared this great unknown they were heading into could become a huge task. Were they up for this visit? Sidnei supposed they were here after all to really check things out. Yes, they could do this visit.

They reached the rental car center and picked out a car, a jazzy red Jeep. Then the trek across town began.

The drive to her parents' house was quiet. Sidnei found herself softly humming snippets of jazz classics she had heard growing up. She kept their beat while lightly tapping her fingers on the armrest. Closing her eyes, she pictured her parents dancing. Funny, though—she couldn't recall her parents ever actually dancing together. She sighed and opened her eyes. They were almost there.

Turning into the block where her parents resided, the heat visibly sizzled up from the sidewalks. With one exception, the yards were made up of scattered pebbles and a desert plant here and there. Her parents' yard had browning grass and a lone shade tree. The house itself was huddled behind the tree.

"Well, here we are," said Logan.

"It's all so brown," said Sidnei in a quiet voice.

Sidnei stepped out of the car into a lineup of ants moving one by one across the driveway. The ants led the way to the front door, which still had a Christmas wreath on it. Sidnei remembered this very same wreath from her last trip here years ago. It was faded and fringed now, probably from lengthy exposure to the desert's elements. The screen door was pockmarked with numerous tears and sagged in the middle. Sidnei told herself that her parents had been using the entrance from the garage and had just overlooked their front door. Still, her mom had always religiously changed the wreath for the season. Sidnei tried to stuff her thoughts away.

Sidnei took a deep breath, received a quick hug from Logan, and tentatively knocked on the door.

"Door's open. C'mon in." It was her father's voice. He sounded far away.

Sidnei and Logan entered the living room. The blue furniture was vaguely familiar, but the dust, the dust. It made Sidnei sneeze.

"Is that you, Sidnei? You're not coming down with a cold, are you?" Her mom, too, sounded distant.

"No. Be right there," said Sidnei. She mouthed the words "Where are they?" to Logan, grabbing his hand.

They continued down a long, narrow hallway. Again, it was familiar—the glass shelves, the country knickknacks—but so dusty. Cobwebs too. A dining room chair was stuffed in the corner, its legs broken. And no music. That was odd. As far back as Sidnei could remember, music always played in her parents' houses.

Sidnei stopped. She held on tighter to Logan's hand and whispered, "Maybe we should have contacted the police first. This is like a crime scene from one of those detective shows on TV, like *Law and Order* or *NCIS*. Broken furniture, the mess and clutter, the disarray. What will we find at the end of this hallway? I'm a little scared."

"I know, but we agreed the police might compound things. Your parents are here though. They're talking to us. We need to see them before we make any rash decisions," whispered Logan.

Sidnei couldn't help but notice that Logan's other hand held his cell phone at the ready. They moved forward.

Just beyond the kitchen sat her parents in the open family room. Sidnei now clutched Logan's arm as she took in the scene.

Her mom sat in a dirty, faded blue recliner, staring at a widescreen TV mounted precariously on top of a bookcase. At least Sidnei *thought* it was her mom. This woman had totally white hair that shot up in tufts from her scalp. Sidnei's mom had entertained an array of hair colors and hairstyles but most definitely not gray, let alone white. Her dad always said she looked just like a movie star. This woman in front of her wore no makeup, and her skin was sallow, with wrinkles flaring in every direction. Sidnei's mom would never have been seen without makeup. Her dad liked having his girl all dolled up. The woman's clothes were baggy and covered with food and milk stains. Sidnei's mom was always dressed up, always. Her dad bragged about how good she looked all the time. Sidnei quickly wiped away a tear as her eyes moved to this woman's nails. Her fingernails curled up a good inch beyond her fingers. Her toenails were actually poking holes in the sneakers she wore. Sidnei's mom never, ever missed her weekly manicures and pedicures. Sidnei caught a sob before it escaped her throat. She wanted to turn away. Her mom was nearly unrecognizable. The overpowering odor of urine filled Sidnei's sinuses.

"Mom, how are you?" asked Sidnei, feeling a little dizzy.

"Oh, Sidnei, we're so glad you have come. But gosh! I've been so sick, upset to my stomach. Knee hurts, of course, all the time," said her mom as she reluctantly pulled her gaze away from the TV.

Yes, this sounded like her mom, but … Her mom had always been impeccably groomed and smelled like roses and lilacs. This woman stared at her blankly. Well, that wasn't necessarily different.

Sidnei leaned over to give her mom a hug. Once again, the distinct smells of urine and dried food filled her senses. Her mom clung to her for a few moments. Sidnei felt nausea bubbling up but hoped she could breathe through it. She loosened her arms, straightened, cleared her throat, and moved toward her dad.

Logan had gone over to her dad to shake his hand. There had been quick hellos. Logan stood back to let Sidnei greet her dad.

"It's good to see you, Dad," said Sidnei.

"You know I can't see worth a damn anymore," said her dad. He stared straight ahead, not blinking. That old glint was now a faint, murky, almost lifeless gaze.

Sidnei bent to give him a kiss on his bald head. She couldn't help but notice how thin he was. He had always been a big man, muscular and athletic. His nails had not been attended to in a long, long time. His clothes were worn but not filthy like her mom's. The dad she remembered, however, would never have worn old clothes. He always said clothes should make a good impression, a statement. He continued to stare straight ahead.

Sidnei pulled herself up and asked, "What's that buzzing sound?"

"Damn flies! Garvan had to come in through the sliding glass door the other night and ripped a hole in the screen. Got no air-conditioning, so we have to put up with the flies. Garvan says it can't be fixed."

"Well, how about if I have Logan look at it? You know he's always been pretty handy," said Sidnei as she winked at Logan. "In fact, I'll just step out with Logan to take a look at things."

Sidnei and Logan made a quick escape to the backyard. The grass had dried up. Remnants of vegetation stood sadly along the fence line, withered and dead. The patio furniture lay in heaps of twisted metal and broken glass.

"You okay?"

"No, but I'm determined to appear to be," said Sidnei. She took several deep breaths, planted her hands on her hips, made one more sweeping appraisal of the backyard, and returned inside.

"So, Mom and Dad, looks like you've been having some pretty hot weather," said Sidnei.

"Yep," said her dad. Her mom just nodded.

"Has Garvan been around much?" asked Sidnei.

Logan made a coughing sound while he tinkered with the sliding glass door and screen. Sidnei sent him a quick glance.

"Oh, Garvan lives with us now. He takes care of us," said her mom.

"Hmmm. Will we be seeing him?" asked Sidnei. She looked from one parent to the other.

"Nope," said her dad.

"Now, Gabe, you don't know. He might be in and out, he said." Her mom squirmed a little in the recliner as she shared this information.

Sidnei quietly sighed. Nothing really out of the ordinary in their responses, and yet not ordinary either. However, their personal appearances and the condition of their home were so unlike what she had grown to expect, it was way beyond scary.

"Zelly is supposed to meet us here tomorrow morning. How about if I just straighten up a bit?" asked Sidnei.

"Not necessary. Your mom has everything perfect like always," said her dad, still staring straight ahead without even a blink.

Sidnei's eyes swept the room. A hard lump settled in her throat. Crumbs littered the carpet and flooring. Stacks of papers, mail, and flyers were everywhere. The upholstery was filthy. Dust and cobwebs covered everything. Sidnei had to stifle a gasp before she responded. "Okay. Then I'll just check the fridge and cupboards for snacks. You guys still like your snacks, right?"

As she moved to the kitchen, Sidnei motioned for Logan to come back inside.

"What do you think, Logan? Do we need to go shopping?" Sidnei asked as she opened the refrigerator door. Besides swatches of mold on the inside walls of the fridge, there rested a partial loaf of white bread, an almost empty jar of peanut butter, and a carton of milk, which, judging by the smell that assailed her, was probably past its prime.

"Looks like I can probably fix the door, Gabe. I'll need to go to the hardware store. And it looks like we need to go to the grocery store too."

Sidnei had stopped breathing for a few seconds when she opened the pantry door. She peered at empty shelves. Only a few crumbs and a couple of dead ants could be found.

"Sure could use some cookies around here," said her dad.

"You got 'em! Anything else?" asked Sidnei.

"Maybe some ice cream, chocolate for me and strawberry for your dad," said her mom.

"Okay! We won't be gone long. Either of you need anything before we take off?" asked Sidnei.

"No, no. You just go," said her mom, her eyes once again focused on the TV screen.

Sidnei and Logan made their way quickly to the front door and exited even faster. Logan had the car down the driveway and on the street in seconds.

Starting to cry, Sidnei choked out her words. "That was so wrong, so very, very wrong. They're two different people. They're ... I don't know, like people you see on the news. They're befuddled and befuddling. And the silences and dismissals are worse than ever. It all feels like smoldering ashes."

"I know, Sidnei. I think we need to poke around a little this evening when they're asleep. Your dad acts like he's not tuned in, but as I watched him from outside, he's taking it all in."

"Since when did Garvan start taking care of them? In point of fact, he's not taking care of them at all. Why, he's never even been able to take care of himself. Why would Mom say he's taking care of them?" said Sidnei, her tears of dismay rapidly being overtaken by anger.

Sidnei wiped at her face, smearing her mascara. Hiccups erupted from her intermittently.

"We have to think about what we just saw," said Logan. "I think they might not be safe. That back entrance doesn't lock. The neighborhood's deteriorated. There's mess on top of mess."

"Okay, first things first," Sidnei said. "We stock the kitchen, start cleaning the place, fix the door, and get someone in to look at the air-conditioning. What else can we do?"

"We'll be there tonight. We have to be extra alert," said Logan.

"I sure hope Zelly can give us some insight," said Sidnei.

Sidnei's mind was whirling. Should she feel guilty or angry? She was puzzled that over the last few years, her parents never once indicated they might need help. It appeared as though they had shut themselves off from the world outside their family room. And Garvan? Why wasn't he taking care of them, if that was indeed his role?

Sidnei went through the motions as she and Logan moved from store to store. They collected the materials for Logan to repair the sliding glass door and screen. Next, they arranged for an air-conditioning contractor to come to the house the following day. Once at the grocery store, they bought enough food for two weeks, along with disinfectant and bleach.

As they loaded the grocery bags into the back of the Jeep, Sidnei said, "I think I might look into having meals delivered. What do you think?"

"Sounds okay but expect your dad to balk."

"I know, but I just don't know where to begin with all this," said Sidnei. She really wanted to cry.

"I think we do things as we see they're needed, like we're doing now. Remember, your parents aren't necessarily going to be overly appreciative. It doesn't take much to anger your dad."

"I know. I know."

"Okay, we've got everything in the car. Let's go," said Logan. He patted Sidnei on the back.

As they made their way back to her parents' house, Sidnei kept her eyes closed, attempting to clear her mind of dark shadows. Logan, Sidnei was sure, was doing pretty much the same thing, but with his eyes wide open as he maneuvered his way through the Phoenix traffic.

Once back at the house, Sidnei grabbed a couple of bags of groceries and cleaning supplies, while Logan began moving the materials to repair the door to the backyard.

"We're back," said Sidnei as she pushed the front door open. She wondered if that door shouldn't be locked. She also made a mental note that she had seen no sign of neighbors yet.

"About time," said her dad. "Thought maybe you two just took off."

Sidnei knew he was trying to provoke her, as in the days of long ago. It had seldom worked then, and she was not going to engage now.

"No. No. It took a while to get everything. Logan's going to work on the door while I bring in the groceries. Then I'll fix you each a snack before I start dinner."

Sidnei stacked all the grocery bags on the kitchen counter, which was going to need a good scrub, she saw. First, she wiped down the pantry shelves before filling them with cookies, crackers, chips, soups, granola bars, and cereals. After removing the mold and scrubbing out the fridge and freezer, she filled the fridge with milk, cheese, cold cuts, salad fixings, and fruit. She stacked potpies, frozen dinners, and ice cream in the freezer. Before really getting into disinfecting the food preparation areas, Sidnei dished up the ice cream for her parents.

Sidnei watched her parents slowly eat while she scrubbed down the kitchen. They spoke little. Sidnei moved on to prepare the pot roast and root vegetables for the oven. Both parents had their eyes fixated on the TV screen. Their spoons occasionally missed their mouths as a result of their intense staring. Sidnei wanted to scream, "Where are my real parents?" But she didn't. She just watched and wondered. In three years, they had gone from being an active and attractive older couple to zombies lost in a twilight zone of filth and unseemly degradation. Zelly better have answers for her.

Sidnei wandered out to the backyard to help Logan once the roast was in the oven and the ice cream dishes in the dishwasher.

"God! It's hot out here," said Sidnei.

"Sure is. You got everything under control inside?"

"As much as I can for the moment. Is that screen ready to go on the tracks?"

"Yes, ma'am! Here, let's put it up."

They chatted on until they could stand back and look at their handiwork.

"Not bad," said Sidnei.

"Those good smells coming from the kitchen aren't too bad either," said Logan.

They had watched Sidnei's dad shuffle in his seat, heard him clear his throat, and witnessed him tilt his ear to better hear what was going on. Sidnei and Logan smiled, high-fived each other, and returned inside.

"All done!" said Sidnei.

"Garvan said it couldn't be fixed," said her dad.

"Now, Dad, one thing I learned from you growing up was that anything can be fixed if you want it to be." Sidnei looked carefully at her dad.

"You always have been a little too much of a rebel, Sidnei. Garvan may not take well to this."

Sidnei opened her mouth to reply but quickly closed it. She would not be baited. She took a couple of deep breaths before she spoke.

"Dad, it's fixed. The air-conditioning should be fixed tomorrow." Sidnei's arms were crossed in front of her.

"What's that?" said her mom.

"Someone's coming to look at your AC in the morning, Mom."

"Oh, that's going to be super, Sidnei, just super," said her mom. She momentarily looked around to blink at Sidnei.

"Okay, how about if we clear off the kitchen table," said Logan.

Her mom turned slowly around again. "Logan, I was going to ask you to look at those things. We've always been just fine, but lately we've been having some trouble." With that, she turned back to the TV.

"Well, all right, but why don't I put this all in a bag for now. Sidnei and I can sort it out when we get home."

"Sure, sure," said her mom.

"We'll just scoop all of this into a grocery bag," said Sidnei.

Sidnei and Logan slowly placed unopened envelopes, receipts, notices, bills, statements, and other official-looking pieces of paper into the bag. Sidnei sensed there was cause for alarm as they sifted through the items. She couldn't remember ever seeing bills, let alone unopened bills, among her parents' possessions.

"I'll put this in our bedroom. Next to last one down the hall, right?" asked Logan.

Her mom simply nodded.

Sidnei followed Logan down the hall. They entered the bedroom together to find stacks of unfolded laundry lining three of the walls. The bed had been freshly made up though. Sidnei flashed back on Zelly's comment about the clutter she would find. She shuddered. Zelly had certainly been right about that.

As Logan set the bag down on the floor, Sidnei thought she saw something move in one of the piles. Her reaction did not go unnoticed by Logan. Sidnei froze.

"Let's think of this as a camping trip. I can pretty much guarantee there will be no snakes. C'mon, Sid, snap out of it. We gotta work together here." Logan hugged Sidnei.

"I'm good. It's just all so overwhelming."

"I know. What time does the case worker show up tomorrow?" asked Logan.

"Nine." Sidnei closed her eyes and burrowed into Logan's chest. She took a deep breath. "Logan, what happened?"

"I don't know." He hugged her even tighter.

Sidnei heard the wind picking up outside. She knew that meant more dust. Taking a deep breath, she was immediately conscious of the taste of dust and dirt. A good old Phoenix dust storm was disturbing the city again, seeping into everything. She peeked out the bedroom window to view the sky but saw only an ugly brown blanket of dust and fine debris choking out the light of the moon.

Sidnei sat pertly, dressed in her new blue taffeta dress and shiny black patent leather shoes. She beamed at Mr. Miller, her fifth-grade teacher. He was handsome and smart. And he was saying really nice things about her to her parents, who had both come for her parent-teacher conference. Usually, it was just her mom. Mr. Miller was describing how well she did in all subjects and how much she loved learning. It was true! She did!

When her family had moved into the big white house, Sidnei quickly decided to find her friends in books. She read everything. Funny thing, though—the more she read, the more she knew, and the more other kids paid attention to her. Everyone wanted to be her friend. Now her family had moved again, to a place called Pueblo. The new kids liked her just like the last group. She still wasn't all that good at games, but her new friends didn't care. Her dad did, but he didn't play with her much anymore anyway. He spent most of his time with Aiden and Tam. Both of them could play games, lots of them, really well.

Her dad shifted in his seat and cleared his throat. Sidnei, her mom, and Mr. Miller all looked at her dad with varying degrees of expectancy written on their faces.

"So, what you're saying is that Sidnei is becoming an egghead," said her dad.

"No. No. What I'm saying is that your daughter, Sidnei, is a very talented student who excels in every subject in the classroom. If her talents are properly nurtured, she will have a very bright future ahead of her," said Mr. Miller.

"Well, that sounds nice. Now doesn't it?" said her mom.

"Geez, Jezzi, she's just a girl."

"Dad, you keep telling me I'm smart," said Sidnei. Confusion was starting to flood her brain as she looked at each adult surrounding her.

"Look, Sidnei, if you're too smart, the boys won't like you," said her dad.

"Mr. Jepson, please understand that your daughter is the most gifted student I have ever worked with. I believe she will go far in life," said Mr. Miller, confusion apparent on his face.

"What Sidnei will need to focus on in her future is finding a good husband," her dad said firmly as he stood up. "We're done here. Jezzi, Sidnei, let's go. Mr. Miller, thank you for your time."

As the three Jepsons passed through the classroom door, Sidnei paused to look back and wave to Mr. Miller. Sidnei thought he looked kind of sad as he waved back at her, even though he was smiling.

Her dad ushered Sidnei and her mom silently out to the car. Sidnei settled quietly in the back seat. It felt like she had done something wrong, but she couldn't figure out what it was that she had done. Her dad did always tell her she was smart. Her friends thought she was smart too. What could possibly be wrong with being smart? She was going to have to think hard on this.

Her mom looked at her dad and said, "Gabe, we should be proud of Sidnei."

Her dad looked into the rearview mirror at Sidnei to say, "Look, Sidnei, book learning is okay for now, I guess. But you need to look for opportunities to be more girlie."

"What do you mean?" Sidnei asked.

"Your mom will work with you on that," said her dad. That glint was in his eyes, all watery, wavy shots of pale blue.

Sidnei shivered as a "Br-r-r," erupted from her throat, though barely perceptible.

Her mom stared blankly ahead. They finished the drive home in silence. Sidnei got out of the car, went to her room, looked at all the books lining the shelves on her walls, and announced, "Hello, friends!" Wrapped in a warm blanket, she quickly lost herself in a novel and read until she was called to dinner.

During dinner, Sidnei listened to her dad give ball-playing instruction to Aiden and Tam. She watched her mom absently serve up plates of food.

Sidnei realized she liked how her mom always smelled, like lilacs and roses. Maybe that was girlie. She knew her mom liked pretty things, so that could be girlie too. Sidnei wondered when the girlie talk would happen. Before she could excuse herself from the table, her mom asked her to help clear the table. Maybe the girlie talk was going to begin now.

Once in the kitchen, her mom began, "Sidnei, I was very proud of you today. Your dad is too, but he's looking ahead to your future."

"Mom, I'm ten," said Sidnei.

"I know, but sometimes you are a little too bookish. Your dad thinks you need to join in a game now and then."

"Mom, I'm not good at games. Besides, my friends like books too," said Sidnei, feeling more puzzled.

"Okay. Okay. Are any of these friends boys?" asked her mom, now openly frustrated.

"Yes. They're smart boys, not like Aiden and Tam."

"That's not very nice. Aiden and Tam are smart. They're also very good at games."

"But they don't know a lot of stuff. My friends know all about things I know about, like stars, planets, and history," said Sidnei.

Her mom stared at Sidnei before saying, "Well, we can talk some more about this tomorrow. It's bedtime." Her mom turned away to wipe the counters.

Sidnei walked off to bed more confused. Everybody she knew liked her for being smart. Her dad, she knew, knew stuff. Why was it okay for him to know stuff but not for her? What was her dad really trying to tell her? Maybe she could find that girlie information in a book. Her mom didn't seem to know. Sidnei shrugged into her pajamas and grabbed a book to read. Before snuggling into her covers, where she always felt safe, Sidnei looked out her bedroom window. The moon was nearly full and made her smile. She knew the moon would look out for her. Was the moon maybe telling her to shine tomorrow? Done! She read far into the night, forgetting all about needing to be more girlie.

The next morning, Sidnei dressed with extra care and spent extra time brushing her blonde curls until they danced in the sunshine coming through her bedroom windows. When she came to the breakfast table, her dad called her "Sunshine." He added, "Now that's my girl!" Surely, thought Sidnei, she could be smart and girlie at the same time then. Grown-ups always seemed to want to make things complicated.

7

Dinner that evening was awkward. Sidnei's parents came to the dining table reluctantly, saying they never used the table for eating anymore. They now ate in front of the TV. Once all four of them were around the table, there was little conversation. Her parents ate like automatons. At the end of the meal, her mom said it was good. Her dad added that her mom's cooking was better. After they excused themselves from the table, Sidnei watched her parents wander off to bed.

Sidnei and Logan shook their heads over and over again as they cleared the table and whispered their plans for the evening.

"I'm going to look in the file cabinet in my mom's study," said Sidnei thoughtfully.

"Hmmm ... I want to take a look at the garage."

"Hopefully, something will turn up to shed some light on what's been going on around here." Sidnei reached for Logan's hand.

"Now we wait for a little bit," said Logan. They quietly put the last dishes away.

Once soft snoring came from the master bedroom, their plans were put in motion. Heading in different directions, Sidnei and Logan walked determinably to their tasks while keeping watchful eyes and ears open—for what, they weren't quite sure. Each was armed with a flashlight. Logan waved to Sidnei as he entered the garage.

Sidnei eased into her mom's study. It appeared to be cluttered like the other rooms. She remembered that many years ago, her parents had told her they had a will prepared. She also remembered that anything important would be filed in the antique filing cabinet. Sidnei slid the top drawer slowly open. Oddly, given the condition of the rest of the house, the files appeared untouched and were neatly lined up in alphabetical order. *Good old mom and her constant tidying and organizing*, thought Sidnei. The first file was an extensive one labelled "Bank Accounts." It was organized by location and year starting with Tempe—1951, then Denver—1952–1953. When Sidnei saw Pueblo—1959, she realized too many memories were wanting to knock around in her head, too many visions of her standing off to the side. She quickly moved her fingers along to "House Deeds" and located the current deed, pulled it out, and set it aside. She didn't know why but thought it might be important. She closed the top drawer and opened the second drawer. "Legal Transactions" drew her eye immediately, and then her heart froze for an instant. This file was divided into two sections. One was labelled "Gabe," the other "Garvan." Her heart now beating rapidly, she pulled the whole file out. Then she spied the slim file in the back of the drawer that was simply identified as "Wills." She added it to her stack. As she quickly flipped back through the files, "Loans" caught her eye. Strange, thought Sidnei, as she had only seen her parents pay cash for everything. She had always assumed they were pay-as-you-go people. Her dad had always pulled cash from the envelopes he collected over the years.

Sidnei sat down on the floor and carefully opened the "Wills" file. She moved the flashlight mindfully over each page. Both wills appeared to be identical, including the final double-sided single page entitled "Durable Power of Attorney for Health Care." She closed her eyes and then rubbed them carefully. Her eyes were not deceiving her. She, Sidnei Jewell, alone was appointed to make health care decisions for her parents when the other parent was no longer able to. Going back to the "Last Will and Testament," she confirmed she alone had been named executrix of each will. None of her brothers were named anywhere throughout the documents. How could this be? When was she to be informed of these decisions? These wills had been prepared twenty-five years ago, long after she and Logan had married.

Sidnei looked up when she heard automobiles idling outside. She turned her flashlight off. Logan announced in a loud whisper that she had better join him in the guest bedroom. Sidnei stood up, grabbed her stack of files, and carefully but quickly walked to the next room along the hallway. As multiple voices outside were raised, Sidnei and Logan held their breath behind the closed bedroom door.

Sidnei heard loud footsteps outside and could see several flashlights pass by the bedroom window. The garage door entrance to the house was thrown open. Heavy footsteps now marched down the hallway. An angry male voice demanded to know why all the doors were locked.

"Why, Garvan, is that you? asked her mom groggily.

Garvan's voice dripped with contempt as he loudly stated, "I want them out of here!"

"Now, Garvan, you know your sister and Logan are here visiting," said her mom haltingly.

"Shoulda known it was them," said Garvan. He spoke with a distinct western twang.

"I told them all you weren't going to like this," said her dad.

"Like? I don't like her! Rich bitch! Why is she even here? I thought you said she was never coming back," said Garvan. "Get her outa here!"

"Garvan, please," said her mom. There was no mistaking the fear in her voice.

"Look, ol' lady, this is my house. I'm telling you, get her outa here!"

Garvan could be heard retreating back down the hall until he came to the guest bedroom. He punched the door open, causing the wood to splinter. He filled the doorway. Sidnei had not seen him in many, many years. He now loomed before the two of them, a massive man, over six feet tall and nearly three hundred pounds. His graying blond hair dangled in a stringy ponytail down his back. His face was littered with scars. He held a wad of chewing tobacco loosely in his jaw, allowing the tobacco juice to dribble down his chin. Sidnei stared at him in complete terror.

"I want you two out of here! You're not needed or wanted, never have been, never will be."

"Garvan, why ..." Sidnei was having trouble breathing and could barely get the words out of her mouth.

"Don't interrupt me, bitch! Locking me out of my own house! What kind of trashy stunt are you pulling?"

"Me? I could ask you what you're trying to pull here," said Sidnei through clenched teeth.

"I do the talking, not you, bitch!" Garvan took a step forward. His eyes narrowed. His body visibly tensed.

Sidnei opened and closed her mouth. No sound came out. She could feel Logan gently pulling her back.

"You're both scum—slimy, sleazy scum! You hear me! Scum!"

Two scarfed heads appeared behind him.

"Garvan, man, we gotta go," said one of the men.

"Okay! Okay!"

The two men scrambled down the hall.

"I'm telling you, I want you outa here!"

Garvan turned and retreated down the hall and out the garage door. The whole room was filled with the reek of pot, body odor, tobacco, and the stench of beer.

Sidnei collapsed in Logan's arms and held on tight for a few moments. Then she looked up and out the door.

"Is he gone?" whispered Sidnei, her heart thumping rapidly.

"I think so, yes," said Logan as he carefully assayed the hallway.

"Should we check on my parents?" asked Sidnei.

"Let's be sure they've gone. Otherwise, we could risk being shot. I found guns, lots of them. I want to be sure they all leave." Logan reached for Sidnei's hand.

They listened to the vehicles screeching away outside, blaring music vying with loud, ugly cursing.

"We should call the police," said Sidnei. Her shaking was beginning to subside.

"The police aren't going to do anything, I'll venture to guess, since nothing really happened," said Logan.

"I feel threatened. My parents should feel threatened. The peace of all of us was disturbed." Her hands formed into fists, and her skin felt clammy.

"Okay. Okay. You check on your parents. I'll call the police."

"No. We do both together."

"All right. Your parents first," said Logan. They walked hand in hand to her parents' bedroom.

"Mom, Dad, you guys okay?" asked Sidnei, guardedly looking into the dark room.

"We're fine," said her mom, with a discernable tremor in her voice.

"That was just Garvan. We're used to him," said her dad from the darkness.

"Well, I thought that was disturbing," said Sidnei.

"Naw! Go back to bed," said her dad.

"Well then, good night," said Logan, ushering Sidnei by her elbow back to their bedroom.

Logan pulled the mangled door as closed as he could. Sidnei smiled tentatively at him. He then dialed the local police. The call was answered on the second ring. Logan explained what had transpired and then listened to the person on the other end of the line for what seemed to Sidnei an interminably long time. Logan ended the call by saying, "Okay then. Thanks for your time."

He turned to Sidnei. "They said it didn't sound like much of anything. That in the future we would need something more substantial to report. Said they did know the address though."

"That's it?" asked Sidnei, her indignation evident.

"Yep! Just another Thursday night in Phoenix," said Logan.

Sidnei bit her lower lip and shook her head back and forth. She was growing increasingly angry and damnably frustrated.

"You know, I feel like punching a second hole through that door." Sidnei raised her arms and punched the air above her. "Well, at least we can share what we found," seethed Sidnei.

"Guns, rifles mostly, a little ammo. Your dad and brothers hunted, so that won't impress the police. Lots of pills all mixed up. But the officer I spoke to did say he got all kinds of crazy calls about the elderly, including keeping their pills all together in cereal bowls." Exhaustion was seeping into Logan's whole persona.

"Lord!" said Sidnei, her eyes big as bullet casings themselves. "I have their wills." Sidnei pointed to the stack of files on the bed. "I'm named sole health POA and the sole executrix. I also have some pretty hefty files labelled "Legal Transactions" with my dad's and Garvan's names on them." She spoke rapidly and now clutched the commandeered files.

"What the hell has been going on around here?" asked Logan.

Sidnei answered hesitantly, a noticeable catch in her throat. "This is my parents' house, and yet it isn't their house. These are my parents' things, and yet they're not." She looked around the room and then in the direction of her parents' bedroom. "Those people are my parents, and yet … yet they're not." A quiet sob erupted from her throat.

Logan moved toward her, taking the files out of her arms. He hugged her tightly.

"We need to think. I wish that case manager would have given you more information, but maybe this is part of what she wanted you to see. It's not pretty, I know."

Tears trickled from Sidnei's eyes as she said, "This can't be safe for my parents. All that shouting and ruckus, and the way Garvan talked to my mom."

"Let's try and get some sleep. Tomorrow is probably going to be a very long day," said Logan as he led Sidnei to the bed.

They lay wrapped in each other's arms until sleep thankfully carried them away. They slept hard but fitfully, like soldiers under fear of imminent attack.

Sidnei awoke with a start when the sun began to peek through the window shades. Logan was no longer beside her. She could hear the water running in the shower across the hall. Sidnei peeked out into the hallway, assessed the coast was clear, and scampered to the bathroom, quickly closing the bathroom door behind her.

Ugh! The cleanup faeries had not arrived overnight. In the early-morning light, the stains and mess looked even more pervasive.

"Good morning," said Sidnei as she peered into the speckled mirror. Dark, bloated circles of flesh held her tired eyes up.

"Morning! You ready for today?" asked Logan.

"Not quite, but I will be," said Sidnei. She grabbed her toothbrush and began her morning routine. Wishing she could rub this entire experience away, Sidnei scrubbed her teeth until her gums were bleeding.

Logan pushed aside the shower curtain while drying himself off with a stiff towel.

"I am here to tell you, Sidnei Jewell, that we are going to make the best we possibly can out of this day. It's what we do!" said Logan.

"Okay, Mr. Positive! I will try my best!"

"I think it best to work from another site this evening."

"Okay again, good doctor. I'm next in the shower," said Sidnei.

Sidnei's shower was quick. She was pretty certain she had dreamed last night about alligators—or was it crocodiles—emerging from the filthy drains. She dressed even more quickly and then joined Logan as he walked out to the kitchen. The two of them stopped abruptly as they were met by her parents, dressed in the same clothes they had worn the day before. Each was seated in the same seat. Each again stared at the TV screen.

"Morning, Mom and Dad," said Sidnei carefully.

"Morning, Sidnei. Coffee is ready for you," said her mom flatly, never moving her eyes from the TV.

"Thanks, Mom. How about we fix you two some breakfast?" asked Sidnei.

"Naw! We got our peanut butter toast," said her dad.

They did indeed have their peanut butter toast. Remnants had already landed on their shirts, Sidnei noted. As she poured herself a cup of coffee, she was pretty certain it was the same bag of ground coffee from years ago sitting beside the coffee maker. She sighed. It was the same hazelnut flavored coffee she remembered. Sidnei sat her coffee cup down on the counter.

"Well, can we get either of you anything?" asked Sidnei.

"I said naw. Don't need nothin'," said her dad.

"Logan and I are just going to go for a short walk then before your company arrives," said Sidnei.

"Company? What company?" asked her mom, startled, actually looking away from the TV for a moment.

"Why, Zelly, Zelly McNulty, your case worker from Desert Senior Health Services," said Sidnei. A little wave of fear ran through her heart. Had her mom actually forgotten that Zelly was coming?

"Oh yes. Well, that will be nice," said her mom, turning back to the TV.

"See you in a little bit," said Sidnei. Both she and Logan waved at her parents as they walked toward the front door.

Once outside, Logan surveyed the street. "I'm glad you did that. I wanted to walk around the block to get a feel for what's going on in the neighborhood."

"I just wanted to get out of there. The whole place is oppressive," said Sidnei, shading her eyes under the bright morning sun.

"Understood. Start looking for anything," said Logan.

"Like what?"

"Not sure, but you'll know."

They walked along silently, making mental notes as they went and nodding occasionally to each other. There were very few fence gates in place. Multiple vehicles, many in need of repair, littered each driveway. Cigarette butts were everywhere. Deep piles of trash and rubbish overflowed onto the sidewalks. Graffiti appeared on the side walls of a few houses.

The circuit complete, Logan announced, "The entire block has gone to hell."

"It's so depressing. What I don't get is where all the people are. Before, they were all outside all the time, sitting in their garages, watching TV, drinking beer," said Sidnei.

"Not to worry. They're here, probably kept tabs on our entire walk," said Logan. He was doing a quick visual romp of the houses closest to her parents. "There's a new car parked in front of your parents' house. Maybe Zelly's here."

Sidnei ran to open the door. "We're back!"

"Sidnei, come meet Zelly," said her mom.

Sidnei stopped when she reached the family room so that she could scrutinize the situation. Her mom sat with an actual smile while sipping tea from a cup. Her hair was combed, and she wore clean clothes. Her dad sat in his chair smirking as a round-faced, curly haired, slightly overweight woman took his blood pressure. She looked up.

"Oh, hi! I'm Zelly," she said brightly.

"I'm Sidnei. This is my husband, Logan," said Sidnei. She noted Zelly wore no uniform or readily apparent identification.

"Just let me finish up here, and then I thought we could have our little chat in the living room," said Zelly as she made some notes on a pad in her lap.

"You gonna be talking about us?" asked her dad, his gruffness taking over. He stared straight ahead, expressionless.

"I think Sidnei should be caught up on your health issues. That's all," said Zelly.

"You gonna tell her about Dr. Schaaff and how he wouldn't give us our pills?" asked her dad.

"I'm hoping Sidnei can help come up with a solution," said Zelly.

"Humph," said her dad.

"I'll just head on into the living room. Logan, are you going to join us?" asked Sidnei.

"Certainly."

Together, Sidnei and Logan walked to their bedroom to get the file with the wills, then back down the hallway to the living room. They settled in armchairs, leaving the couch for Zelly. As they waited, Sidnei scanned the room. Having learned in a short amount of time that what was once familiar was no longer familiar, she searched for anything out of the ordinary, confirming it all was. Notably, components of the stereo system were missing.

Zelly lumbered down the hall, took a seat in the middle of the couch, and passed her business card to Sidnei. The card identified Zelly as a senior case manager. That didn't tell Sidnei much.

"I wonder if you could elaborate on what exactly you do for my parents," said Sidnei.

"Well, sure, I can give you a little history actually. As you can see, your parents have significantly deteriorated. When I first started looking in on them four years ago, they were vibrant and healthy. They looked like movie stars. The house was spotless. When your dad learned that he had macular degeneration, he was thrown for a loop. He gave it a good fight for a year or so. Then Garvan showed up. Garvan took your dad's keys away, and your dad sat in that chair he sits in today and has not moved far from it all this time. Your mom kept her spirits up for a while. Then one day about a year ago, I arrived to find her sitting in her chair. Her hair had not been combed, no makeup, mismatched clothes on, and she was in the same stupor as your dad," said Zelly.

"Why wasn't I informed of this?" asked Sidnei, her voice filled with incredulity, her eyes filling with tears.

"Well, Garvan said he was the POA. I never knew you existed until your parents were looking through some photo albums. They came across a picture of you, and I asked who you were," said Zelly, looking uncomfortable as she squirmed in her seat.

"Garvan is not the POA. I have discovered that I am. Did you ever ask him for proof?" asked Sidnei, holding up her own evidence.

"Actually, no. Your parents corroborated his claim, so I just assumed he was legit ... legitimate," said Zelly, starting to stammer.

Logan snorted, and Sidnei fired a quick, meaningful glance at him.

"He isn't, I can assure you. Here. Let me show you the paperwork," said Sidnei as she pulled each power of attorney from its packet.

"Oh my gosh!" said Zelly as she carefully looked over each document. "I can't tell you how many papers he has signed illegally." She was openly perspiring. Her eyes were welling up with tears. "There's so much I have to share with you," said Zelly, nearly out of breath and speaking in a whisper.

"Can you tell me why my parents don't have a doctor currently?" asked Sidnei.

"Yes, that's one of the things I wanted to discuss with you," said Zelly. Tears now streamed down her face. "Your parents had seen Dr. Schaaff for years. Then one day, he called me into his office, where he informed me that he strongly suspected that Garvan was picking up their pills at the beginning of every month and neglecting to give them to your parents."

"That's illegal," said Logan as Sidnei concurred by shaking her head.

"Yes and no. So far, I've seen no evidence of Garvan using drugs. I've been to Desert Senior Health Services officials, to Medicare, and to the local police. They all want eyewitness accounts like a videotape. I've spoken to Garvan, who indignantly told me that when he picks up the drugs each month, he brings them home and locks them in a cupboard. When I pointed out that he's often gone for days, weeks at a time, and I wasn't clear how his parents then had access to their medications, he stormed out of the room saying everyone needed to leave him alone. Lately, Garvan has left the pills out. I've tried putting them in pill dispenser boxes for each day, but there are some pills always missing. When I show up a week later, the boxes are in disarray, and even more pills have disappeared or are scattered about the family room. Dr. Schaaff remains staunch in his belief that Garvan is taking the pills even though so far none of us can prove it."

"And what do you think?" asked Sidnei.

"I agree with Dr. Schaaff. Your parents have no visitors anymore, and they certainly don't leave the house."

"I found a whole bowl of pills in the garage," said Logan.

"I'll bet those pills are theirs. Can't we have you or someone check them out?" asked Sidnei.

"Sure, but be aware that that won't prove Garvan is taking them. The elderly often put their pills together for a variety of reasons. With your mom's progressing dementia, who's to say she hasn't been hoarding them?" said Zelly.

"That's absurd! I thought you were on my parents' side."

"I am. I am. The bottom line is that Dr. Schaaff let them go as patients because he doesn't want to get involved." Zelly was wringing her hands to the point of making them red.

"Isn't that unethical?" asked Logan.

"Nothing can be proven, and a doctor may ask for a patient to be reassigned. So, now they must find a new health care provider," said Zelly.

"How long have they been without one?"

"Several months. I've talked to a couple of physicians and could give you their contact information. One in particular might be best for your dad, as he can be rather difficult to please."

"Did you give this information to Garvan?" Sidnei was trying unsuccessfully not to be openly outraged. Her left foot tapped the floor; her right hand massaged her left hand.

"Oh yes. But he told me it was their problem, and they would have to fix it."

"Gabe is virtually blind," said Logan.

"And Mom's mind is going at what appears to be an alarming rate." Sidnei spoke in a raised whisper.

"That's just it. Garvan takes, but he doesn't give back to the right people," said Zelly.

"What does that mean?" said Sidnei, looking perplexed.

"Drugs are disappearing. Food is disappearing. I don't want to think what else might be missing. But keep in mind nothing can ever be proven," said Zelly, misery written all over her face.

"Last night, Garvan and a couple of thugs stormed the house," said Logan.

"And the way he spoke to my mom is unforgivable," said Sidnei with a shudder.

"I've called him on the way he speaks to your mom several times. He just shrugs and stomps away," said Zelly.

"Still, you're saying nothing can be done. Can't we get some people in to monitor?" asked Sidnei.

"That will be expensive, but I can give you some names."

The doorbell rang. Logan looked at his watch and suggested that should be the air-conditioning people. He left the room to greet the people at the door. Together they continued back down the hall to the family room. Logan gave Sidnei a thumbs-up as he steered the repairmen to the back of the house. Muffled conversation could be heard from the family room.

That left Sidnei and Zelly to face off. Sidnei looked directly at Zelly and asked, "Why? Why? Why?" The weightiness of the discoveries, the tension permeating the air, and the ultimate lack of sleep were taking their toll. Sidnei sat slumped, rubbing her forehead. Her left foot continued to tap the floor.

"I don't know, Sidnei. Your parents, especially your mother, seem to think Garvan can do no wrong. This happens far more frequently than you might think. Ultimately, most of these situations turn out hurtful. And again, none of us have definitive proof, but our guts tell us something is very wrong here. I'm hoping you can help us unravel the truth. I'm sorry," said Zelly. She too appeared drained and bewildered.

Looking straight at Zelly, Sidnei shared her thoughts out loud. "It sounds like you know my parents fairly well, and they appear to like you. So, you should know that they won't be very accepting of others they don't know well—my dad for sure."

"Yes, I know. The bottom line is they do need help," said Zelly. She had regained command of herself and rustled through her notebook, pulling out cards and brochures.

Together, Sidnei and Zelly put together a list of meal providers and home care professionals whom Sidnei would contact. They strategized how best to present these necessary services to Sidnei's parents. At the end, Sidnei was determined she could bring some order to the chaos surrounding her.

Returning to her parents, Sidnei stopped Zelly just short of the family room. With a heavy sigh, Sidnei said quietly, "This all saddens and infuriates me. I'll do what I can. I just hope their resistance isn't greater than what I can give."

"Sidnei, I'm so glad I've met you. I'll help to reinforce what you try to do. Now, let's get started."

Sidnei and Zelly found her parents napping. Logan and the two AC repairmen sat at the kitchen table settling the bill. The room, Sidnei realized, was a comfortable temperature.

"Thank you," Sidnei said to the repairmen. "This is a big help."

"No problem, ma'am. Anytime you need us here, just let us know." And with that, the repairmen excused themselves and left.

"Nice fellows," said Logan. "Looks like we have more homework," he added as he eyed the papers and brochures Sidnei was holding.

"Indeed we do. Like you said, we're going to work this out," said Sidnei with a reassuring smile.

"I'll just be going," said Zelly to the room at large. She gathered her things.

Sidnei walked to the front door with her.

"I'm sorry I had to dump this on the two of you, but you're my only hope. Thank you, both of you. I'll be by next week. Let me know how I can help. I'll be in touch," said Zelly. She made her way out to her car.

Once Zelly pulled away from the curb, Sidnei returned to Logan. She plopped in the chair across from him.

"You know how much I love you right now?" asked Sidnei.

"Not as much as I love you!" said Logan.

They both laughed quietly. The laughter helped to ease the very long day.

"I did explain to your parents that we're leaving this evening. They seemed unfazed with the news. Your mom did ask though when we were coming back. She seems a little more with it today," said Logan.

"Well, maybe since Zelly made her look a little more like herself."

"Let's get our stuff together and out to the car while they're still sleeping."

They tiptoed to the bedroom and quickly packed. One trip out to the car was all they needed to get their stuff stowed in the trunk.

Returning to the family room, Sidnei and Logan found her parents waking from their naps.

"It sure is better in here with the air-conditioning back on," said her mom, with a genuine smile.

"Humph," said her dad.

"Mom, Dad, we were thinking you could use a little more help around here," said Sidnei.

"Sure could. I just can't keep up with it anymore," said her mom.

"Oh, you do all right. I don't want any strangers in here," said her dad.

"Dad, how about if we start with someone taking you to the doctor after I get a new one set up for you?" asked Sidnei, trying hard not to hold her breath.

"Same person could maybe pick up groceries for you," said Logan.

"Well, I guess that could be okay," said her dad. "Damn Garvan never has a vehicle."

"I was also thinking having lunch delivered during the week might be good," said Sidnei, still trying to breathe naturally.

"Don't want any damn chicken or fish."

"I know, Dad. When I set the lunches up, I'll tell them." Sidnei took a long, even breath.

"That sure sounds nice," said her mom.

"Okay! That's where I'll start tomorrow," said Sidnei. She looked at both parents, whose gaze never wavered far from the TV. She took another deep breath.

"It's about time to go," said Logan.

"All right then. Let me just hug you guys."

Her mom clung to Sidnei for an extra moment. Her dad waved off her hug. Logan shook hands. And then Sidnei and Logan walked down the long hallway and out the door.

The sky was clear, but the air was laden with dust. Sidnei could feel it seeping into her sinuses, permeating her skin. As she slid into the front passenger seat of the car, she looked vainly for the outline of the moon before closing her eyes.

Sidnei gazed at the big sky surrounding her in the midst of the wheat fields in eastern Colorado. Stretching from the horizon to infinity, the sky was as blue as a robin's egg. Sidnei thought it was kind of like a big old blanket she could hide under with the sun and the moon taking turns as her companions. While she felt small in the immense blue landscape that surrounded her, she couldn't help but smile from ear to ear. Sidnei patted the neck of the animal beneath her, a tall, muscular, dappled gray gelding. She was riding a horse—and riding it well, she was told. In fact, she was riding better than Aiden and Tam.

Her cousins had given her specific horseback riding instructions throughout the weeklong visit. Sidnei now knew how to use the reins to control and guide her horse. She also knew how to use her voice, hands, and legs to let her horse know what she wanted it to do. Most importantly, Sidnei was not only mastering this skill set, but her cousins said she looked like she had been riding forever, just like them.

She was in command of an animal considered an athlete in its own right. This particular horse had actually won races locally. It tickled her to think that this horse was way bigger than any old ball Aiden and Tam threw around. And she, Sidnei, was in charge of this big, beautiful creature.

Reining in her horse to stop, Sidnei saw the grown-ups gathering around the pool off in the distance. Grown-ups got more confusing as she grew older. At the age of thirteen, she was becoming skillful at reading their rages and playing their good sides. What Sidnei wanted more than anything was to be a grown-up herself, independent of older grown-ups' whimsical moods. She especially knew she needed to stay out of the sights of her father. Most of the time, he didn't think she did anything right. The only way she knew to please him was to look pretty and keep moving out of his way. Weird how those cheerleaders at his high school could get away with acting all dopey around him. If she behaved like them, she would be yelled at for being inappropriate. However, now she just might be able to capture his attention with this new discovery that she was a natural rider. But did she really want that attention? Would he even pay attention? Would she be setting herself up for further rejection? After all, she was still just a girl to him. This, she knew from almost everyone around her, was only a small part of who she really was. Her academic prowess caught everyone's attention. Except, of course, her dad's.

As the horseback riders picked up their pace and neared the grown-ups, Sidnei saw that glint in her dad's eyes. *Oh boy!*

"Sidnei, Aiden, Tam, we're taking off soon. You need to help untack and cool down the horses. Then we're off," said her dad as he looked over the riders.

"Okay," said Sidnei, patting her horse as she slipped gracefully to the ground.

She gave her horse a hug and periodically gave him water to drink as she worked her way through his cooldown. Aiden and Tam, she noticed, still got help with the cooldown from the cousins. Sidnei gave her horse one last hug and a carrot and then turned to walk toward her parents.

"Sidnei, we've been hearing all about your good riding this week," said her mom, pride evident in her voice.

"Thanks, Mom! I've had fun. It is sort of like a game, and I can really do it," said Sidnei, a little breathless.

"Now, Jezzi, don't get her all riled up about this. Horseback riding is expensive, and we just can't afford it," said her dad. He was steering his family to their car as he waved to the relatives behind him.

"But, Dad, everyone said there are ways to pay for lessons, like helping with the horses," said Sidnei. Her eyes were beginning to narrow. Her smile was long gone.

"Well, we did see how well she did with the cooldown," said her mom quietly.

Her dad quickly cut both of them off by saying, "No daughter of mine is going to work at a barn. She needs to use her time to keep herself spruced up."

Resigned, Sidnei crawled into the back seat and sat quietly all the way home, lost in her thoughts. She was going to make this happen. The fact of the matter was, she mused, that she had learned to do her own thing and to do it with little visibility. Even now in the car, her dad, Aiden, and Tam talked about ball games and did not recognize her existence. Her mom stared out the side window, her mouth drawn in a straight line across her face. Sidnei drew her arms tighter and tighter around herself as she began to formulate a plan.

Once home, Sidnei unpacked and then searched the phone book for riding stables. There were a couple closer to her house than she would have thought. She copied their addresses and phone numbers and made appointments for later in the week. When the rest of the family attended ball games, Sidnei went off to interview for volunteer positions at each of the two stables. One was more than happy to work around the schedules Sidnei presented, which were Aiden and Tam's schedules for ball playing.

Soon after starting at the stables, Sidnei couldn't help but notice the extensive garden the stable owners kept in a separate fenced area. The vegetables were all plump and lush. When Sidnei asked about the garden, the proud gardeners gave her a tour and offered her some yummy samples. Sidnei went home that afternoon with a very big idea, a very good big idea. She knew there was plenty of room for a garden in their backyard at home. It turned out all she had to do was ask.

"Mom, you know the place out back where the grass doesn't grow so well?"

"Yes." Her mom, as usual, was dusting and scrubbing. She didn't even look up.

"Well, I was wondering if I couldn't start a garden there. I would prepare the soil, plant some seeds, and take care of the plants myself." Sidnei was smiling from ear to ear when her mom finally stopped and looked at her.

"If you really want to try, go ahead. You're going to have to really work with the soil out there."

"Oh, don't worry. I'll read up on it, and it'll be great. You'll see. Thanks, Mom!"

Sidnei skipped a little as she went off to the garage to gather digging tools for her gardening adventure.

Sidnei tackled the new garden project with zest. Her parents never commented on what she did during her afternoons. Long ago, Sidnei had learned that if they didn't ask, she didn't need to tell. Her parents were at Aiden's and Tam's practices and games when she was at the stables, and neither of them wandered out to her garden. Did they know what she was doing? Sidnei was so busy she couldn't give this much thought. With the garden project, she could now wear jeans more often, even on afternoons when she wasn't working and riding at the stable. On those afternoons, she became an unlikely gardener at home, and a darn good one to boot. Her after-school attire was earthy and always a little dirty. She did change for dinner when she knew her dad would be home. All the exercise gave her a trim figure and color in her cheeks. Her mom shook her head in amazement, and even her dad appreciated the fresh vegetables she harvested. He even said she was pretty from time to time. Sidnei found herself squirming from the intense looks he gave her on those occasions, his glint a bit discomfiting.

Still, Sidnei smiled a lot now, for her riding skills just got better and better. Exercising the boarded horses had quickly become her primary task at the stable. Recognizing her skills as a rider, the stable owners freely offered Sidnei instruction. Between school, riding, and gardening, Sidnei was growing in confidence in many arenas, not the least of which was to become an independent woman. She gave horseback riding lessons to handicapped children once a week. She entered her vegetables in the local fair competition and won prizes. As long as she showed up for dinner, she knew her family members would never ask what she had been doing.

Now, when she contemplated the moon at night, Sidnei radiated an energy of which she was not yet aware, but many others around her surely wondered what was different about her. In many aspects, she had managed to free herself from those physically and emotionally constricting parts of her life. Yet hard as it was to try to figure out her parents and their reluctance to allow her talents to be fully realized, she loved them. They made sure she had everything she actually physically needed. They made sure she had pretty things. Although they didn't seem to realize it, they were making it possible for her to achieve the independence she needed to become her own person. Weirdly, Sidnei was coming to appreciate that they were helping her more than they would ever know.

9

Ninety minutes later, Logan announced that they had arrived at the resort. Sidnei opened her eyes to gaze at a breathtaking view of the mountains and Paradise Valley. She slid over to Logan, fell into his arms, and sobbed. Together they leaned into each other for a long, long time. Finally, Sidnei pulled away, took a deep breath, and let it out slowly as she eased out of the car.

"It feels like this nightmarish madness has lasted eons," said Sidnei, wiping at her eyes. "And this," she said, making a sweeping gesture with her hands, "is so beautiful, a beautiful dream."

"I decided what we needed was a good relaxing shower, a good dinner, and a good night's sleep." Logan led Sidnei to the reception area where they were greeted with smiles and treated to glasses of champagne.

As they were escorted to their suite, the contemporary but rustic decor, mingled with the magnificent views of the Arizona mountains, had an immediate calming influence. Those same views continued from their suite with its wraparound patio. The mosaic tiled shower quickly beckoned, where the two of them held each other for yet another long embrace. Dusk began to settle in, and they dressed for dinner at the on-site restaurant for exceptionally prepared farm-to-table cuisine. During dinner, Sidnei outlined her plans for the two of them the next day.

"I went back over my notes and the literature Zelly gave me. So, I have our tasks for tomorrow divided up."

"Okay. What are my tasks?" Logan took a sip of wine as he sat back in his seat.

"First, check and see if we can get a late checkout time so we can work from this lovely place." Sidnei looked up from her list to smile at Logan.

"Consider it done." Logan smiled back.

"Then see if you can get the outside of my parents' house cleaned up."

"No problem."

"And didn't you say all the locks need to be changed?"

"That I am eager to do!"

"Me? I'll call the Agency on Aging and see if they can provide any assistance. Zelly seemed to think that was where I should start. And I really want to get meals delivered and to get someone in there to check on them in between Zelly's visits, as well as help them out a little."

Logan leaned across the table and took Sidnei's hands. "All sounds good! Now, let's enjoy the meal and the view."

When they returned to their suite with nightcaps in hand, they found the outdoor soaking tub had been prepared for them. It offered a soothing end to the day.

Sidnei woke early the next morning, slipped out of the bedroom, and was hiking Camelback Mountain fifteen minutes later. When she returned to the suite, Logan had a huge mug of coffee waiting for her. Sitting out on the patio and enjoying the view once again, Sidnei went over the items they had discussed over dinner the night before. She made separate lists for the two of them, adding names and phone numbers and other pertinent pieces of information she could glean from the items Zelly had given her. She sat back to take a long sip of her coffee and absorb the amazing view.

"You know, I think I'm ready to do this now. Yesterday, it was all so overwhelming. And the scene with Garvan … I know there will be more of those. What I don't understand is why all of this is happening at all. I feel like I've truly lost the parents I knew before." Sidnei put her coffee mug down and nibbled on a croissant.

"I don't know either, but I'm ready to get started. I did arrange for a late checkout while you were on your walk, so we can work from here through the day. Our plane doesn't leave until ten this evening. What's my next assignment again?"

Sidnei handed Logan a short list. He moved inside. She chose to begin her list from the patio. Her first call was to a representative of the local Agency on Aging. She explained the situation her parents were in to the representative. He promised to send a care coordinator out to talk with her parents. However, he informed Sidnei that the agency's funds were currently frozen and that her parents would probably have to be placed on waiting lists for any services for which they might be qualified. Feeling dismissed, the familiar bubbles of frustration were beginning to resurface. Sidnei ended the conversation knowing that her parents could very well ignore the phone call to set up this interview. Okay, she had had no preconceived notions that this was going to be easy. Her parents needed two basic things at this time—food and someone to look out for them. Maybe the food delivery would be easier to set up.

Sidnei scoured the information Zelly had given her regarding meal deliveries in the area. Her call to the local Meals on Wheels service resulted in another waiting list explanation. Good heavens! Originally, she had thought a restaurant near her parents' home that offered home delivery to seniors would be expensive. They were not government affiliated, however, so maybe it would be a more fruitful conversation. A friendly voice answered the phone.

"Hello. The Cafe. How may I help you?"

"I'm Sidnei Jewell. My parents are in need of meal delivery service. I was told you might be able to help me."

"Of course. We offer meal service Monday through Friday with an extra salad on Fridays for the weekend. Do your parents have any food allergies or restrictions?"

"My dad won't eat chicken or fish."

"Not a problem. We're a restaurant, so we can tailor our meals for our clients' preferences. You know, if you have time to come over for lunch today, we have a few reservations open. You could sample the food yourself."

This was too good to be true, thought Sidnei. She made the reservation and went off to find Logan.

Arriving at the restaurant, they found it to be upscale with reasonable prices. The food was amazing! They each ordered something they thought might appeal to Sidnei's parents, shrimp and pasta. It took no time for them to sign the paperwork to initiate the meal delivery. When dessert, a luscious chocolate-cream pie, arrived, Sidnei thought she might cry. This was indeed too good to be true.

With coffee, Sidnei learned that Logan had had immediate success with his first phone call.

"How did your morning go?"

"It was great! I found a crew to clear the debris around your parents' house. Got a pretty good price too. Then I talked to a locksmith about replacing the outside locks. He had a pretty good suggestion. He recommended a lockbox in case some emergency should come up. A key to the house is put in the box, so the fire department can get in. Actually, the fire department puts the lockbox on the front door. You complete some preliminary paperwork and arrange to be there when the guys from the fire department install it. What do you think?"

"Sounds good to me."

"He also mentioned looking into a medical alert system."

"That's the thing seniors wear on their wrists or around their necks?"

"Yep. The alert system notifies the police or fire department if they fall. Your parents are pretty out of it, so maybe ..."

"I can't see either of them wearing one of those things."

"Still, it's probably something you should talk to them about. What do you think?"

"I'm going to do just that, think about it. I also think I need to get back to my list. I know you have some work phone calls to make. As pleasant as this has been, it's time to move on."

Sidnei went into the afternoon hoping to find a home care agency that could check on her parents once or twice a week, take them to doctors' appointments, and monitor their medications.

As Sidnei started to explain the situation to the first agency she contacted, the person on the other end interrupted. "Ma'am, the seniors may choose to accept the service or not. It sounds like your father may not be welcoming. If that's the case, we'll pull our caregivers from your parents' home."

"But I've met with their case manager from Desert Senior Health Services, and she'll tell you my parents need assistance."

"We can't give what isn't wanted."

"But it's needed whether they want it or not," said Sidnei.

"Seniors have a right to decide what's best for them," said the person on the phone.

"But my dad is blind, and my mother is struggling with dementia. They can't always make good decisions for themselves or by themselves," said Sidnei, now frustrated.

"Again, the final decision rests with the seniors themselves."

Sidnei was aghast, but she knew the phone call was going nowhere. She simply responded, "Okay, thank you," and ended the call. She took a deep breath and let it out slowly.

Fortunately, the next agency she called had a different perspective. They recognized that not all seniors made decisions in their best interests and that some could be a little difficult. This agency worked with these more problematic seniors to best serve them and to meet their needs. Sidnei found herself holding her breath during this conversation. She now exhaled.

"So, you'll take on my parents?" she asked.

Logan was giving her a thumbs-up from across the room.

"Oh, yes! We like challenges. They make our days go quickly."

"Thank you! I think I might cry," said Sidnei.

"No need. We'll take good care of them. As soon as you can reach them, give us a call, and we'll go right out to set everything up."

Sidnei looked at her watch. It was 3:00 p.m. They had a 10:00 p.m. flight to catch to DC. She had a few more hours yet to pull her efforts from the day together.

After dialing her dad, Sidnei was surprised when he answered on the first ring.

"Dad, this is Sidnei. I just got off the phone with an agency that will help you out a little," she said, her excitement evident in her voice.

"Now, Sidnei, I don't want any strangers in my house," said her dad.

"Dad, we already talked about this. The people were very friendly on the phone. They're prepared to do a little cleaning, help you get to appointments, and take you grocery shopping."

"They better be strong and good-looking."

"Now, Dad." Sidnei grimaced.

Her dad had handed off the phone to her mom, who said, "Oh, Sidnei, I'm so excited! You made my day!"

"That's fabulous, Mom! A man named Randy is going to come by to ask the two of you some questions and get to know you. He'll be calling you before he comes, so stay by the phone. Okay?"

"Okay."

"Also, The Café is going to start delivering meals to you Monday through Friday, just as soon as you tell me when you want them to start. Isn't that great?"

"Oh my," said her mom.

"And Logan has some people coming to clean up outside."

Sidnei heard her mom starting to cry. "Now, Mom, you need to just sit back and let these people all help you and Dad."

"Oh, I know, Sidnei. It's so nice of you." Her mom choked a little on her tears.

"Mom, we're happy to do it. Now we had better get off the phone, so these people can contact you. Please take it easy, Mom," said Sidnei, fighting back tears herself.

"Thank you, Sidnei. Thank you." The phone went dead.

Sidnei massaged her forehead. "Dad might be a problem," she said in the direction of Logan.

"I would be surprised, although pleasantly so, if he wasn't," said Logan. "We better make our final calls and get moving to the airport."

Settling into her seat on the airplane, Sidnei pulled her Iceland notes out. It wasn't long before she closed her eyes, and before she knew it, the plane was landing.

As they made their way home, Sidnei couldn't shake a growing sense of unease. Her stomach gurgled; her heart burbled. When she got home, she made herself a cup of tea and went out to her gardens, searching for the moon. It narrowly sliced the night sky, leaving it almost totally shrouded in darkness. She was feeling woozy when she went to bed. Her dreams had become increasingly troubling over these last few days and grew more so on this night.

10

Sidnei let herself in quietly through the front door, gently shutting it behind her. As she hung her jacket on the hall tree, she licked her lips. Salty—must have been the popcorn she and her date had shared at the movies. Smiling, she looked in the rooms flanking the central staircase. Like always, there was no one there. Her friends told her stories about their parents waiting for them to return home from dates. Her parents let her come and go pretty much as she pleased. It actually would have been weird to find either one of them waiting for her.

She started up the stairs and then stopped. Muffled voices were coming from her parents' bedroom. Sidnei was pretty sure her mom was crying. Moving slowly, silently up the stairs, Sidnei stopped just below her parents' door and listened.

"Gabe, no! We'll have to move again," said her mom, sobbing.

"Now, Jezzi, it's not the end of the world. Look at how many times we've had to move, and you've been fine," said her dad.

Sidnei sat down on the step where she had been standing. She put her arms around her knees and rested her head between them.

"Gabe, the kids … we can't keep moving them," said her mom, now sniffling.

"They'll be fine. They're always fine," said her dad.

"Gabe … Sidnei …"

"No, Jezzi, we have to move. They allegedly have proof this time, but they won't press charges if I surrender my teacher certification," said her dad, speaking softly.

"What? You've always said you didn't do any of those things! No! No! No! What will you do?" Her mom was now wailing.

Sidnei frowned into her lap as tears slid down her face. She didn't understand the conversation, but her whole being was sinking. What exactly had her dad done?

Her mom was again sobbing. Her dad kept repeating, "It'll be okay. You'll see."

Sidnei pulled herself up and tiptoed to her room. Once inside her room, she fell onto her bed and used her pillow to muffle her sobs. Slowly, Sidnei returned to her waterfall. It usually made her feel safe, but now it made her frightened of what was on the other side. She bit her lip to keep from crying out loud.

When Sidnei came to breakfast the next morning, she found her dad making pancakes. As he cooked, her dad was delivering the familiar "opportunity speech" to her brothers. Sidnei silently took her seat, nibbled at the stack of pancakes set before her, and then left for school with her brothers. Nothing was said to her. Her dad never even looked in her direction.

Life went on as usual for a few days. Then her dad announced at dinner one night that they would be moving to the Denver suburbs soon. Her mom remained silent. Her dad and brothers chattered about what schools would have the best teams.

Sidnei asked to be excused, stood up, and went for a long walk. She would be entering high school not knowing anyone. Her horseback riding was probably over. Her science experiment at school would be left unfinished. She had scoured the newspapers in the school library, but she found nothing about her dad. What was she looking for? What had he done? Was it something unlawful? That night, her dad said he had to leave his job because of something he had done. If this news hadn't made the papers, how bad could it be? She kept moving. After five miles, she found herself back at the house, just another house to walk away from.

11

After a fitful night of sleep, Sidnei awakened to an early-autumn chill in the Pennsylvania air. Her morning walk was brisk. Sitting at her desk now, Sidnei took in the rabbits, birds, and chipmunks vying for the birdseed that flew from the bird feeder nestled among the pines off the gazebo. The songbirds perched on the feeder and dropped birdseed that was quickly scarfed up by the bunnies on the ground. The chipmunks would make speedy dashes along the pine branches to brazenly snatch birdseed from beneath the songbirds' feet. Sidnei was rooting for the birds.

She turned back to her computer. Using her parents' account number, which Logan had found in the paperwork they brought home with them, and correctly guessing her mother's password to be her birth year, Sidnei opened their account transactions. She ran through several screens a few times, stood, and then called Logan, pacing as she waited for him to pick up.

"Oh good. How soon can you come home?" asked Sidnei. She felt a chill come over her. She had stopped pacing and stood staring at the computer screen. "Okay, I'll wait. I don't want to talk about this on the phone, so I'll wait to show you what I found. No, no, that's fine. You should finish up there. I'll need you to focus on what I found when you get here. See you later."

Sidnei sat down and went through the screens again. There was no doubt about it. Her parents had been paying their bills on time until about six months ago. Over those six months, increasing amounts of money disappeared near the beginning of each month. The last three months, all their deposits were removed from their account in large cash withdrawals, shortly after each check was deposited. Her parents had continued to write checks for the house payment, utilities, and credit card bills. However, each of those checks bounced, and extra cash withdrawals continued, resulting in rather sizable overdraft charges.

Sitting back, Sidnei closed her eyes. Surely the bank had tried to contact them. But maybe that was one reason they didn't answer the phone. Sidnei shook her head. That bag of paperwork in Logan's office upstairs, she was now assuming, had to have further information for her. Another chill ran through her body. She sat transfixed by her computer screen until dusk when she heard Logan's car pull into the garage.

Logan came right to her, and together they looked at her parents' account as Sidnei walked Logan through her findings. Side by side, they went upstairs and began to sort through her parents' paperwork, making separate stacks for house payments, utilities, credit cards, and medical expenses. The findings were grim. The house was in foreclosure, and her parents would soon be evicted. The utilities would all be cut off at the end of the month. Credit card payments were all in arrears, a couple of cards completely maxed out. And, of course, Sidnei and Logan already knew about the doctor situation.

Sidnei started to cry. "Logan, this is all so very sad. Why … why didn't they say anything?"

"I'm not sure they even understand their situation," said Logan. Sidnei thought he actually looked more angry than sad. "Look, Sidnei. We're going to help them now, but based upon a few of our first encounters, I would venture to guess this won't be easy. You're going to have to be strong for them and for me."

"Okay," said Sidnei, wiping her tears. She stood up and pulled her shoulders back as she announced, "Okay. Okay. I'm going to call Dad."

Sidnei looked at her phone, thinking, *Please, please, please make him answer.* She punched the numbers in quickly.

Immediately, a gruff hello responded.

"Hi, Dad! It's Sidnei. Please don't hand the phone to Mom. I have to talk to you."

"All right, all right." The characteristic grumble in his voice did not escape Sidnei.

She took a deep breath before she began. There was no sense in walking around the issue. "Dad, Logan and I have been going through all the papers we brought home with us. It seems someone has been removing cash from your bank account at the beginning of each month. Then there hasn't been any money left to pay your bills. In fact, cash withdrawals continue throughout each month, resulting in some hefty penalty fees."

After a long pause, her dad answered in measured tones, "Well, there's only one person that could be. I'll talk to him."

"Dad, he seems kind of explosive. Maybe someone should be with you when you speak to him."

"Naw, Sidnei. I'm used to him." And with that, her dad hung up.

Sidnei looked at Logan, who could only shake his head. He walked over to Sidnei and gave her a hug.

"I have to admit I'm frightened, Logan," Sidnei said as she looked up at him.

"Me too. Me too. Let's go out to eat and plan our next attack over drinks and dinner."

"You're right. We need to step away from all this for a moment in order to reset, or maybe reassess, our approaches," said Sidnei. Her voice was tentative as she stared at some unspecified spot ahead of her. She wanted desperately to retreat to her waterfall, but she knew that would not help Logan. Instead, she made a call to Chez Arlette and was able to secure a reservation within the hour.

Once seated at a quiet corner table, Sidnei and Logan put their heads together in conspiratorial fashion.

"I know there's no sense in asking why again and again. So, I think it's best to find a way to get my parents out of this mess." Sidnei absently moved the food around on her plate. Her eyes met Logan's as she leaned across the table.

Logan leaned in too. "Well, we've made a start on doing just that."

"Yes, but how do we keep their money from disappearing?"

"You're going to have to call the bank."

"I know. I need to know what interaction they've had with my parents, especially in recent months. And Garvan. Dad all but said flat out that it was Garvan who's been siphoning their funds."

"You need to be careful around the topic of Garvan."

"I know that too. But I can't figure him out. He's certainly not taking care of my parents." For a moment, Sidnei's gaze appeared to be directed at someone or something far, far away.

"Try to stay focused on your parents."

"I know. I know. I know. So, here's the plan. One, I call my dad to see how he did with Garvan. Two, I call Mom and Dad's bank. I can't imagine that their bank can't help somehow."

Sidnei raised her glass to Logan. He raised his glass as well and said, "May the night bring some light to shine on all this tomorrow."

The next morning, Logan went off to work, and Sidnei began to execute her plan. She first called her dad to see how things had gone with Garvan. Not surprisingly, Sidnei learned that Garvan denied everything. In fact, Garvan insisted that her mom had given up doing the bills. Here, Sidnei added that her mom had never given up paying the bills. She had indeed continued to write out checks to pay the bills just like she had always done. There quite simply was no money to pay the bills because it had been removed from the checking account after it was deposited.

To all this information, her dad simply said, "Harrumph! Garvan said he didn't do it."

"Dad, someone's pulling your money out. The next step is to notify the bank and the police, so I'll—"

"Now wait a minute! Let me talk to Garvan again." Her dad hung up.

Sidnei called the bank anyway. The first person she spoke to at the bank put her on hold while a bank manager was consulted. A voice returned to inform Sidnei that her parents were longtime customers and that, as a result, the bank had to honor all cash withdrawals. It was their policy.

"Excuse me, but I'm looking at their transaction history for just the last three months, and the cash withdrawals are way out of character with my parents' earlier banking history," said Sidnei.

"While that may be true, it's also plausible that their obligations may have changed."

"I would really like to speak with someone in person. This activity appears highly suspicious to me."

"Your parents will have to come in themselves. I'm not finding your name on any of the accounts. The account you're referring to is actually in a trust."

"A trust? My parents are pretty infirm," said Sidnei.

"That's our policy. You'll need to bring them in." The voice was growing edgy.

"Fine! Will ten o'clock Thursday work?" asked Sidnei.

The appointment was set. Sidnei made her next call to the airlines to arrange a flight back to Phoenix.

After securing the flight, Sidnei's thoughts flew. Was she jumping to conclusions? Why would Garvan think he could get away with all this? And the drug issue too! What did he have over their parents that necessitated them handing their independence to him? Just how ill were her parents?

The final thought put her back into action. She called the office of the doctor Zelly had recommended and made appointments for her parents in three weeks. That call was relatively easy. She knew the paperwork she would need to complete was on its way.

Sitting down with a hot cup of tea, Sidnei let her eyes close. Visions of envelopes and the sounds of guarded whispers and hushed giggles took over. Taking a deep, deep breath, Sidnei sent these negative images away. What did they mean anyway? She found herself shivering. She knew she had to keep her mind clear in order to be alert to what was going on around her. She had to be strong, not distracted, like Logan had said. Opening her eyes, Sidnei took a sip of the tea and held her face over the teacup to savor the scent and the warmth. She slowly drifted toward the waterfall in her mind, albeit briefly. She accepted that she had to be strong.

Moving to the sun porch, Sidnei gathered her notes for her Iceland trip. She was soon immersed in descriptions of the northern lights, apertures, and camera settings. Here, she felt sure of herself. It would not be long before she would see what the dark sky could bring to her.

12

Sidnei's dad was now in marketing. Seldom home, he returned laden with bottles of liquor and rarely carried a basketball. The mysterious envelopes she had seen passed to him over the years were now bigger and fatter when they appeared. They were delivered by attractive young women who appeared eager to speak with her dad. Her mom never sat in for these conversations. Her mom had had another baby boy, Garvan, who ate up most of her time. The little time her parents did share together, they spent going to Aiden and Tam's ball games.

The move back to Denver had not been all bad. Sidnei was placed in all accelerated classes, so she quickly found new friends with common interests and goals. One guy, she especially liked to talk to. In fact, he had asked her out to dinner this evening. Sidnei found herself taking extra care with her hair and clothes for this date. She braided her hair into a french braid and had purchased a classic little black dress, hoping to look sophisticated.

When Sidnei heard the doorbell ring, she took the steps two at a time. She smoothed her dress and opened the door. She flashed a smile at this new guy, Logan.

"Wow! Sidnei, how many layers of brilliant and beautiful are you?" said Logan.

Sidnei blushed. "You don't look so bad yourself, Logan Jewell. Let's go."

"I'd like to meet your parents." As Logan said this, Sidnei watched as he took in the sweep of the entryway.

Sidnei felt mystified for a brief moment before she responded, "They're actually out, attending my brothers' games."

"Well then, let's go," said Logan. He held the door for Sidnei and followed her down the sidewalk to his car.

Dinner was at a fancy restaurant, which neither Sidnei nor Logan had any experience ever visiting. Sidnei was a little in awe as different members of the waitstaff bustled around them, pouring water, handing them menus, and delivering a basket of breads. She surreptitiously looked at the nearby tables to see what the other restaurant patrons were doing. When the waiter came to ask about other drinks, she was ready.

"I'll have an iced tea, please." Sidnei sat up straight.

"Me too," said Logan.

"And may I ask you to describe the beef bourguignon?" Sidnei focused all her attention on the waiter.

As the waiter described the luscious meal, Sidnei smiled at Logan. The waiter said he would return with their iced teas and to take their orders. Sidnei now looked at the cutlery flanking the stack of serving dishes in front of her. Looking quickly at the tables to the right and left of her, she thought she might have gained some valuable information.

"Looks like you start from the outside. So, this must be the salad fork."

"I know my mom puts out two forks when company comes for dinner," said Logan.

"You're right." Sidnei carefully took in Logan and all those surrounding them. "This is fun, and I just know it will be delicious."

The waiter returned and took their orders—a salad and the bourguignon for Sidnei, a salad and steak frites for Logan. Sidnei insisted on sharing an order of profiteroles for dessert.

When the food began to arrive, the two of them did surprisingly well figuring out the silverware order and the multilayered place settings.

"Whew!" said Sidnei. "This is really, really good. Did you ever take the international foods class?"

"No."

"You should. Or how about that modern problems class?"

"Why don't we both sign up for it?"

"That would be fun." Sidnei looked at this young man sitting across from her. She believed she could talk to him all day.

Then Logan sent a cherry tomato flying when he was cutting his steak.

They both grinned as Sidnei quietly told Logan to leave it and to act like nothing out of the ordinary had happened.

The egregious tomato remained under the table as they pushed back their chairs and prepared to leave. Sidnei and Logan agreed that if the tomato had ears, they would be burning as the two of them talked and laughed about it all the way back to Sidnei's house.

Logan came around to the passenger door and opened it with a flourish. He offered a hand to Sidnei, which she accepted. They slowly walked up to her front door.

"I had a great time tonight. I've never been to a fancy restaurant before," said Sidnei.

"Neither have I."

They both laughed. At the door, they turned to face each other. Sidnei studied Logan's face. The stars seemed to be sparkling in his eyes. She quickly averted her own eyes. Logan left Sidnei with a gentle kiss on her forehead before she opened her front door and went inside.

Quietly as always, Sidnei made her way up the stairs. Soft snoring and the baby's gurgling came from her parents' room. Sidnei dressed for bed and then worked on homework until her eyes were fighting to stay open. She turned out her light and fell sound asleep almost immediately. A couple of hours later, a knocking sound awakened her.

"Sidnei." The knocking persisted. "Sidnei, I believe this one outside is for you," said her dad. She heard her dad walk away from her door and close his own bedroom door.

Kneeling on her bed and looking out at the yard below, she saw Logan. The full moon cast a spotlight on him as he strummed away on a toy guitar, singing a popular love song very much out of tune. He looked up at her with a smile, brown curls falling over his forehead and pausing to bite his lower lip before continuing his song.

Sidnei's heart did a little pitter-patter as she blew him a kiss. She dressed quickly. Tiptoeing past her parents' door, she stealthily made her way down the stairs and out the door. Logan was beside his car, holding the passenger door open. Sidnei curtsied and settled herself in the seat.

"Good evening," said Sidnei. She looked at Logan mischievously.

"Hi!" He smirked back at her.

"How did you know I could get away?" Sidnei looked at Logan with big eyes.

"You seem to do whatever you want. A good hunch, right?" Logan started up the car.

"Yep! So, where are we going?"

"An adventure. Just sit tight and enjoy the night sky."

Logan maneuvered efficiently through the late-night Denver traffic and headed into the mountains. They talked about solutions to calculus problems and write-ups for chemistry labs. Sidnei was now quite certain she could talk to him forever. It seemed he was interested in everything she was. When they stopped for gas, both looked up and marveled at the stars overhead. Venus sparkled brilliantly among the stars.

As dawn approached, Logan carefully parked the car. He handed Sidnei a blanket, a bag of groceries, a small sketchbook, a map, and a compass. He carried a cooler and a fishing pole. A short walk brought the two of them alongside a stream where they sat on the blanket and watched the sun rise in glorious shades of pink and orange.

"I love the sunrise." Sidnei hugged her knees as she snuck a side glance at Logan.

"Me too! And I'm starving! Prepare for the best breakfast of your life!"

Logan started a fire and then prepared bacon and eggs. It all smelled so good that Sidnei found herself salivating. Logan served up the eggs and bacon with freshly squeezed orange juice. Sidnei took in the crisp, fresh air perfumed by the smell of an open fire and the aroma of bacon, the rippling stream, and this guy who made her feel so comfortable.

"It is delicious and—all right—probably the best breakfast I've ever had!" Sidnei licked her lips and then smiled. "You are too much!"

"You're not bad yourself, Sidnei Jepson. Let me just clean up these dishes and put stuff away."

"I can help too, you know."

"No, no, this is my treat today." Logan winked and got to work.

Sidnei watched Logan wash and pack everything. She watched his hands, his muscles flex under his T-shirt, and she watched the mystery that was him. Was this really happening?

Logan then sat beside her with the map and compass in hand.

"I was thinking you could do a little hiking and exploring, which I know you enjoy, while I fish for a while. Now, let me get you started with the map and compass. The trail you'll follow is pretty well marked, but just in case, you know. Right now, you're here, so orient the compass to the map like so. Zero the compass, turn the dial to the left, lay the compass on the side of the map like so. Every so often, just pull out your map, put the compass on the map, and turn until the needle is in the doghouse."

Sidnei giggled. "Logan, I've used a compass before."

"Oh, well, of course you have. So just don't get lost." Logan looked up, and they both laughed.

"It looks like we're going to be able to see each other most of the time anyway. It's pretty open here." Sidnei looked in both directions.

"Okay. Okay. Two hours."

As Sidnei set off down the trail, she wondered when she had told Logan how much she liked to hike and take long walks. Someone had actually listened to her. She smiled as she made her way along the trail. There was so much to see. She had seen pictures of the lark bunting before. Here along the trail, the bird fluttered up from the grasses. Its canary-like song bubbled and trilled on the air. The bird blended well with its surroundings, dressed in its new streaky brown winter garb. The butterflies were a magnificent purple. Sidnei was pretty sure they were hairstreak butterflies who had to be on their way south. The grasses were a marvel as they moved in the wind, showing their blue underskirts. Sidnei put her map and compass in her pocket and twirled around to take in her surroundings. She clapped and squealed. And in her spinning, she stopped when she sighted Logan casting with rod and reel off in the distance. His lush brown curls fell over his forehead. It was as close as she had ever come to watching living poetry, she thought. She brought her hands to her heart and continued to watch. Then she sat and sketched all she had seen.

At the end of the two hours, Sidnei made her way back to Logan. She had many things to describe. Logan held up a string of trout for her to admire as she walked toward him.

"Looks like a good morning for both of us!"

"Let me clean these, and then we'll take off."

Sidnei sat beside Logan as he prepared the fish. She told him about the things she had seen and shared her sketches—although not the sketches of him.

On the drive home, Sidnei fell asleep. Logan nudged her when they pulled up to her house. No one appeared to be home at Sidnei's. After all, it was Saturday, and Aiden and Tam had practice and games. As Sidnei removed her things from the car, she guessed that her family had assumed she was out for one of her early-morning hikes. Logan came to her side of the car and helped to gather her things. They held hands as they walked slowly up to her door.

"Logan, this has been an amazing night, an amazing morning. I can't thank you enough." Sidnei looked him straight in those sparkly eyes of his.

"It was fun! Don't know how I can top it, but I will sometime. Guess I'll see you Monday."

"Monday. Yes." Sidnei still held Logan's gaze.

Sidnei leaned in a little, and Logan kissed her tenderly. He turned and walked down the sidewalk. Sidnei waved as he drove away. Smiling, she turned to go in her door, thinking life went on, but oh how exciting hers had become!

13

Less than a week after she flew out of Phoenix, Sidnei flew back in. Her thoughts tangled, she made the drive across town on autopilot. Pulling up to her parents' house, her heart ached. She stepped out of the car, pulled her shoulders back, and placed one foot in front of the other. Sidnei let herself into her parents' house, announcing her arrival once inside the front door.

"C'mon in! You know the way." Well, her dad had grown no less grumpy in her absence.

A gasp stole her breath away for a moment as she began to walk down the hallway. Sidnei could not get used to all the dust, cobwebs, clutter, and debris. She knew she would have to stay focused on the goals she had set for this trip. Taking one big breath, she entered the family room with smiles and hugs for her parents. Sidnei stood between her parents and began to explain the primary reason for her visit.

"So, Mom and Dad, we need to visit your bank this morning," she said, looking back and forth at each of her parents.

"Now, why is that, Sidnei?" asked her dad, although his attention never wavered from the TV.

"I explained this to you over the phone. To begin cleaning up the money issues for you like you've asked, we have to find an alternative way to route your money," said Sidnei.

"Humph."

"We have an appointment at your bank in an hour. Both of you have to be at the appointment since both of your names are on the account. Then I thought we would go out to lunch. After lunch, we'll come back here to meet with Randy, who's organizing your caregiving services, and later with Mariah, who oversees your meal delivery service."

"About those meals. They're pretty skimpy," said her dad.

"Gabe, they're wonderful! We haven't had food like that in a long time," said her mom, her attention finally diverted from the TV.

"Okay. Well, we'll talk about all of this after lunch. How about if you two start getting ready," said Sidnei.

"Oh my! I don't know, Sidnei. My hair … my nails," said her mom.

"Let's take you back to your room and see what we can do." Sidnei helped her mom to her feet. They made their way slowly to the master bedroom.

Sidnei was behind her mom as they stood at the master bathroom mirror, both peering at a woman Sidnei still barely recognized.

"I was wondering, Mom, when did you stop coloring your hair?"

"Oh, Garvan said I was too old to be doing that. It just sort of went by the wayside," said her mom wistfully.

"You know, your new caregiver can always take you to your beauty shop. Just say the word. It will be my treat."

Her mom started to cry softly.

Reaching out to touch her mom's shoulder, Sidnei quietly said, "Mom, I'm here. Let's do this step by step. Next step right now is freshening you up and getting clean clothes on you."

Once that was accomplished, Sidnei picked out a clean shirt and shorts for her dad and went to check on him. She found him cursing his shoes as he looked up when she entered the room. "That you, Sidnei? I never can get these damn things on." He dropped one shoe and then the other as he tried unsuccessfully to meet a shoe with a foot.

"I tell you what. Let's get you into some clean clothes and then I'll help you with those shoes," said Sidnei. She found herself gritting her teeth.

Sidnei had never had children of her own, but she was pretty sure getting her two parents ready for the trip to the bank was not unlike getting preschoolers ready for a similar trip. Once she had them dressed and—she thought—ready to go, her parents informed her that they couldn't leave the house without their canes. Finding the two canes amid all the clutter was a challenge. Then moving them out to and into the rental car was another challenge. Sidnei was perspiring, and her parents were growing cranky. Sidnei secured both her parents in seat belts. As she got into the driver's seat and buckled her own seat belt, she could not stop thinking: How many more times today would she have to do this? It was a lot of work. *Whew! Giant baby steps! Giant baby steps!* She missed Logan. She had assured him she could make this trip on her own. She glanced in the rearview mirror to make sure she was still smiling. Yes, she was smiling but also perspiring. Damn!

The bank was less than ten minutes away. It took another ten minutes to get her parents out of the car, situated with their canes, and settled in chairs inside the bank. Sidnei just kept smiling and chatting until the bank manager came to introduce herself.

Reaching out to shake Sidnei's hand, the bank manager said, "Hi! I'm Ms. Lopez. I believe we spoke on the phone. We'll need to move over to my office."

Sidnei shook hands and identified herself. She took each parent separately to a seat in Ms. Lopez's office. Dropping into the third seat, Sidnei sighed. She was fully aware that every eye in the bank was on her and her parents.

"Let me begin," said Sidnei. "As I explained on the phone, my parents' finances have spun out of control in recent months. Their funds are disappearing at the beginning of each month …"

Her mom looked bewildered as she looked at Sidnei, then the bank manager, then Sidnei's dad. Interrupting Sidnei, she hysterically interjected, "Gabe, we should be just fine. We've always been just fine. When the money comes in, I pay the bills just like always." She began to cry.

"I know, Jezzi. I don't understand it," said her dad as he reached out to pat her mom's knee.

Looking directly at the bank manager, Sidnei continued, "So I need their funds to be accessible by me, so I can pay their bills and monitor their funds."

"Well, as I explained over the phone, their money is in a trust," said Ms. Lopez, holding up one hand when she saw Sidnei preparing to speak again. "You will have to open another account with all three of your names on it and transfer the funds to that account each month."

"Why can't she just add her name to our account?" said her dad.

"The trust you initiated with us is only in your names. Since this is a legal document, we would have to have the court approve any changes. It's easier and more timely for everyone to have you open a new account with your daughter's name on it," said Ms. Lopez.

Her mom kept her head down. Sidnei could hear her quietly sniffling.

"Mom, Dad, let's get this done. Okay?"

"Okay, but I don't understand," said her dad.

Her mom continued to look dumbfounded, but her tears were clearing up.

Ms. Lopez pushed papers over to Sidnei, which Sidnei carefully skimmed and then signed. She turned to her parents and guided them through the paperwork and where they should sign, reinforcing that in order for her to oversee their finances, this was the easiest way to do it for a while.

Ms. Lopez asked Sidnei to come with her to pick out checks while her assistant brought Cokes to her parents. Once out of her office, Ms. Lopez led Sidnei into another office.

"Ms. Jewell, I would like to introduce my boss, Mr. Rubens," said Ms. Lopez.

"A pleasure, Ms. Jewell! It's a fine thing you're doing for your parents. I've known them for many years. I haven't seen them much the last few years. It looks like they've fallen on hard times," said Mr. Rubens, looking Sidnei square in the eye while shaking her hand.

"Thank you, Mr. Rubens. I'm still very confused about my parents' situation. I do hope you understand the urgency of my request."

"Indeed. Sometimes our senior customers do fall into the wrong hands," said Mr. Rubens as he indicated Sidnei should take a seat in front of his desk.

Sidnei said, "I've spoken to the police, and they would like a video of what I spoke to them about. I don't suppose you could show them your ATM transaction footage."

"Unfortunately, no, not without a court order. I can tell you that typically in these circumstances, the seniors will say they gave permission to the person accessing the ATM machine with their pin. Then we can't act, as I'm sure the police explained to you. It happens more often than you might think. I'm sorry we can't offer more help. With this new account, though, as long as you move your parents' money as soon as it comes in, it should be much more secure." Mr. Rubens sat back in his seat, seemingly satisfied.

Sidnei took a moment before she replied. A tight lump had formed in her throat. Why was this so hard? "I appreciate what you're letting me do. However, I need to be sure the person who's pulling out my parents' money cannot do so just on a whim. The overdraft fees are significant."

"Your parents are longtime clients of ours. It's our policy to allow such loyal customers to take money out when they need to," said Mr. Rubens.

"Even when there's no money in the account? That makes no sense." Sidnei could feel her heartbeat increasing, her anger seething from deep inside her.

"We have found with our loyal customers that it always gets caught up," said Mr. Rubens, tapping his fingers on his desk.

Sidnei stood, towering over Mr. Rubens, her voice rising. "My parents are no longer able to do this. They live on a fixed income. *They* are not pulling out their funds; someone else is. Since that's happening, they're not able to pay their bills, including the mortgage from this bank. You're telling me that you will not help these longtime, trusted clients of yours. Shame on you! I'll bet this third person who freely accesses my parents' account laughs every time he draws money out of their account. Where's your humanity? This just isn't right! Thank you for at least taking the time to meet with me."

Sidnei turned and walked out of Mr. Rubens's office. Ms. Lopez quickly escorted Sidnei back to her office, where the appropriate papers were reviewed, a new account was created, and a new checkbook was issued.

Mr. Rubens waved from his office as Sidnei carefully moved her parents out to the car. Sidnei did not wave back.

Once they were settled in the car, Sidnei proposed that they go to the seafood restaurant just a block away. She remembered that this had been one of their favorite restaurants. She was using every last bit of restraint to not start shouting.

"Oh, Sidnei, that would be real nice," said her mom. Sidnei thought that just might be a real smile on her mom's face. That smile was the calming influence she needed right then. Sidnei took a deep breath and pulled the car out of the bank parking lot.

"Okay with me," said her dad. There was no mistaking the genuine smile on his face.

"Great!" said Sidnei with a smile of relief. The restaurant was just around the corner from the bank. She pulled into a handicapped parking spot by the front door.

As Sidnei helped her mom out of the car first, a waiter came out to assist her mom from the car to the first table right by the door. This allowed Sidnei to return and carefully maneuver her dad out of the car. Once again, Sidnei got voluntary assistance. There were people who were trying to help, she had to admit. She thanked them graciously before helping her parents with the menu.

Both her parents ordered plates of shrimp scampi and popcorn shrimp with iced tea. They ate ravenously, quickly clearing their plates. When the waiter suggested dessert, her parents ordered strawberry shortcakes and devoured them as well. Sidnei watched in awe. They appeared to be starving.

She made a mental note to check the fridge and pantry when she got them back to their house.

Now schooled in getting her parents in and out of the car, Sidnei was able to move them back to the car with minimal assistance from the restaurant staff. She had them safely in their chairs back at their house in no time.

Randy from the caregiving agency arrived shortly after their return. He had met with her parents once before, and they thankfully seemed to like him. They all agreed to two morning visits per week to take care of doctor visits, some shopping, a little cleaning, and incidental needs as they came up. Sidnei was pleased. Her dad actually talked, rather than grunted, with Randy.

Mariah's visit was a little different. Her dad groused about the portions, then complained about the selections. Mariah made suggestions. Her dad countered. Her mom, on the other hand, just kept saying, "Now, Gabe, it's just fine. It's just real nice." Sidnei had to give Mariah credit for hanging in there with her dad.

It wasn't until Mariah left that Sidnei was able to check out the fridge and the pantry. They were practically bare. She tried not to gape.

"Uh, Mom, Dad, the groceries I bought you last week … they seem to be pretty much gone."

"Oh, Garvan had a poker party. He put on quite a spread," said her mom.

Taking a deep breath, Sidnei said, "Well, it looks like I need to go to the store. Why don't I do that now. When I come back, I'll have some ice cream with you. How does that sound?"

"Sidnei, you're doing too much," said her mom, though her eyes did not move from the TV.

"Ice cream and maybe cookies sound good," said her dad.

"Okay, I'll be back in a bit," said Sidnei as she gathered her purse and her keys.

Sidnei shut the front door behind her and then took a deep breath. She looked around. She was going to find Garvan. He had to be near. She could feel him, smell him. Easing the car out into the street, she looked to the right and to the left, turned the corner, and then parked. This house on the corner had people going in and out, she had noticed. Maybe the people inside knew where Garvan was. Sidnei knocked on the door.

"Yes?" The person answering the door was tall, thin, middle-aged. His eyes shifted to different points and then focused on Sidnei.

"Yes. Excuse me, but I'm looking for Garvan Jepson and was wondering—"

"Just a minute." He partially shut the door. Sidnei heard muffled conversation from the back of the house. Then the door burst wide open.

"What do you want, bitch! I told you to go. I don't want you here. Nobody does." Sidnei backed up a bit. She couldn't seem to make her mouth move.

"That's right! Back up, turn around, and leave. That's what you always do anyway." And then Garvan laughed, a laugh that scraped and cut at her heart.

Her words came tumbling out. "Garvan, you're letting our parents die. You evil son of a bitch! You take their drugs, their food, their money, their dignity! I hate you!" Others in the house were peering around Garvan's shoulders.

Garvan loomed before her and laughed again. His sheer bulk was intimidating, his odor noxious, and the white dust around his nostrils terrifying. "Get the hell out of here! You heard me, bitch. Out of here!" The door slammed in her face.

Sidnei stood perfectly still, barely breathing. She looked around her. No one, nothing moved. It was just hot and dirty. She made herself take a few breaths, turned, and moved to her car. Her hands shook on the steering wheel for several seconds. She had to go shopping. That's what she said she was going to do. She had to stay focused and do what she said she was going to do.

Pushing thoughts of Garvan out of her mind, she started the ignition. Driving out of her parents' neighborhood quickly brought her to a more prosperous area. She did her grocery shopping there, buying all the things she knew her parents liked. She even bought a bouquet of flowers for her mom.

Arriving back at her parents' house with her purchases, she put the groceries away, served up the dishes of ice cream, and put the bouquet in water, delighting her mom. She found the phone number of her mom's beauty shop and arranged to have her mom's hair colored and cut on a day when the caregiver could take her. With her parents napping, Sidnei picked up her mom's purse and her dad's wallet, both lying out in the open. Sidnei removed their credit cards but could find no debit cards that could be used at the ATM. She also could not find her dad's driver's license. She tried not to imagine what Garvan might be doing with these. It had indeed been a full day.

As her parents were waking from their naps, Sidnei was putting the finishing touches on their chef salads for their dinner. She explained that she would be returning to take them to their appointments with their new doctor in a few weeks. She hugged them goodbye and went out into the dark desert night. Where was Garvan at this moment? She shuddered. A lone guy shrouded in a dark hoodie stood on the street corner smoking as she turned off her parents' street. Garvan maybe? The guy raised his head and laughed, a laugh she could not mistake. She knew to keep driving naturally until he was out of sight of her rearview mirror, but that did not stop her scream. Her hands shook, her heart beat rapidly, and her tears fell. She made it to the resort but had no idea how she had driven across town.

Entering her suite, Sidnei walked quickly to the armchair and sat down. And she breathed, until she could feel her breath returning to normal. She called the police to report the incident with Garvan. Not surprisingly, the police dismissed her as hysterical over nothing. Now, she could call Logan. He answered on the first ring.

"Logan, I …" Sidnei's tears returned in earnest.

"Sidnei?"

"I ran into Garvan, and he and I …" In between her tears, she relayed her confrontation.

"Okay. It sounds like you're safe. You're safe?"

"Yes. Yes, of course. But he's vile and evil and mean." Sidnei's tears were subsiding a little. "I did get my parents to the bank. They were no help really, but the new account is started. We met with Randy and Mariah. Those visits were okay. But when I went to check my parents' cupboards and found them empty, I went a little crazy. I know I said I would keep Garvan out of my trip, but I just couldn't. Later, I found their credit cards but not their ATM cards. I took the credit cards."

"It sounds like you did fine."

"Yes, but I'm worried. Garvan can still get their money."

"Should be harder though."

"I know, but how will he treat my parents when it gets harder? No one seems to want to help."

"You try to get some sleep tonight. When you get home tomorrow, we're going to brainstorm this like crazy."

"I love you." Sidnei closed her eyes and imagined Logan's face.

"And I love you. Now get some sleep."

"I'll try."

Before Sidnei went to bed, she had room service deliver a light meal. Then she double-checked to be sure all her doors and windows were locked.

This probably wasn't necessary, she knew, but she had to feel safe. From her safe haven, she looked out at the night sky. The stars and planets were all out. The moon was a little bigger slice tonight. She studied this view while munching on her meal and sipping a glass of wine. After a while, it occurred to her that everyone was actually excusing Garvan. Why? There were so many questions to be answered.

14

Sidnei awakened to the sounds of birdsong and to the splendor of the sunrise. It was her sixteenth birthday. What special things awaited her today? she wondered. Taking special care in preparing for the day, Sidnei arrived at the breakfast table truly radiant. There she found only her mom, who was studying the grocery ads.

Without even looking up from the newspaper, her mom reminded Sidnei, "Don't forget you're to pick up Tam from practice today." Hearing Garvan fussing upstairs, her mom got up and hurried up the stairs.

"Okay," said Sidnei as she looked around the empty breakfast table. "Guess I'll just be going to school then," she said to no one in particular.

Once at school, Sidnei received many birthday wishes and hugs. Her friends had her favorite cupcakes, chocolate with chocolate icing, to celebrate at lunchtime. Logan gave her a beautifully wrapped golden box, which he explained she could not open until he picked her up on Saturday. He was quite sure she would not be able to guess what was inside, so he was taking the box back and was not entertaining any guesses as to its content. She would have to remain in suspense for the next two days.

Later, returning home with Tam in tow, she found no one else at home. She did find a note on the fridge asking her to heat up the spaghetti for Tam's dinner. After dinner, she helped Tam with his homework for a while until she began her own homework. At nine o'clock, she sent Tam off to bed and went upstairs to her room, where she continued with her homework. As she was preparing for bed, she heard the front door open, her mom shushing the baby.

A short while later, Sidnei's mom burst into her room and announced, "Here. Your dad said you should have this." Her mom exited the room as quickly as she had entered it. Garvan was crying nearby.

Sidnei walked over and peered into the shopping bag that had been left on her bed. At the bottom was a tissue-wrapped item. Sidnei carefully pulled it out of the bag and unwrapped the tissue paper. A white sweater. She held it up. It was a long-sleeved white cardigan, as simple and plain as could be. Sidnei found herself quietly asking, "Does anyone wear these anymore?" Catching her reflection in the mirror, she tried to imagine this sweater with the outfit she wore, apple-green bell bottoms with a matching bubble blouse and purple espadrilles. Sidnei carefully folded the sweater back into the tissue paper and placed it back in the shopping bag, which she put in the back of the closet. As she prepared for bed, she squeezed her eyes shut a couple of times, vowing not to cry. She sought out her happy place with the beautiful waterfall.

Waking early on Friday, she left for school before anyone else was up. She focused all her attention on her classes and aced all her Friday quizzes. When she got home, she had an early dinner with her mom and brothers before they all left for Aiden and Tam's games. Sidnei talked on the phone with Logan for about an hour before she went to bed. She knew Saturday would be special.

Rising Saturday to a day filled with sunshine, Sidnei dressed in jeans, a T-shirt, and sneakers as Logan had requested. She fixed herself a bowl of cereal as her family members prepared for another round of practices and games for Aiden and Tam. When the doorbell rang, Sidnei's mom reminded her that she had to be home for dinner, as her dad would be back from his business trip.

"Okay. No problem. Back at six," said Sidnei as she walked to the front door.

Logan greeted her on the porch with a quick kiss and a hearty, "Let's get going!"

"Are you going to tell me where we're going?" teased Sidnei.

"Nope! Just prepare for the surprise of your lifetime!" said Logan.

They chatted about school and classes as Logan drove them outside the city limits and into the countryside. When he turned down a country road toward a horse farm called Country Downs, Sidnei could not contain her excitement.

"No! This is too much!" Sidnei's smile stretched from ear to ear.

Logan pulled his package from Thursday out from under his seat. "Better open this now," he said.

Sidnei ripped open the box and carefully read the card inside. "One day of horseback riding with your best friend. XO, Logan."

"Logan, I'm about to begin the best day of my life! Wow! Thank you!"

Placing a big, wet kiss on Logan's forehead, Sidnei jumped out of the car and ran to the stable area. Logan followed. A young man came to meet them with a handsome appaloosa, and Sidnei stopped short. *Wait! Yes! It is! A dappled gray gelding!* Sidnei gave Logan a quick hug. She talked briefly to the trainer, who handed her chunks of carrots. Petting the gorgeous gelding, Sidnei fed him carrots and talked to him in a low voice as she beamed at Logan.

Together, Sidnei and Logan rode all over the expansive farm acreage. When it came time for lunch, Sidnei spied a shady sycamore tree and declared it a perfect setting. As they ate sandwiches and brownies, they talked about what their futures might bring.

"What do you think you might want to do after graduation next year? I, for one, want to travel far and away." Sidnei stared off into the distance.

"Always the dreamer," said Logan.

"No, seriously, I want to put a backpack on and hike all over the US, then maybe Europe." Sidnei's voice had dropped, and her eyes were closed. "I have imagined this a thousand times." Sidnei now had a vision of a sad Mr. Miller from long, long ago. She shook her head to make the vision go away.

"And college? You're the smartest kid in school."

"No. No. That's not for me. At least not right away. I need to see some places, do some things, take some pictures, meet some people."

"Golly, I was thinking you would go to CU with me."

Sidnei reached for Logan's hand.

"No, I have to get away. You, on the other hand, have to stay. How else are you ever going to get that PhD in chemical engineering that you're forever talking about?"

"These pictures you'll take … will you send some to me?"

"Of course. You'll get a copy of every picture I take of the moon and the planets and the sunrise." Sidnei reached for Logan's other hand, and they slowly stood. "I'll be back, but right now I'm thinking I want to get away."

They held hands, looking intently at each other. "And right now I want to ride that beautiful gelding as far as we can go."

"You're on!" said Logan. Together they packed up their lunch things. They kissed, and then they were off to the farthest reaches of the farm.

When Logan returned Sidnei to her home later that afternoon, he brought an even more confident young lady, supercharged with possibilities. This had been a day to remember. Sitting down at the dinner table that evening with her fully assembled family, it was Sidnei who spoke first. "How was everyone's day?"

They all stopped to look at her. One by one, they answered. "Fine." "Okay." "Good." "Sure, good." Garvan just stared at her. Then they turned to each other and talked about what they usually talked about.

Sidnei just smiled. Her sixteenth birthday celebration that day had been truly wonderful.

15

It was less than a week since her last visit to Phoenix. And here she was in New York City preparing for her flight to Iceland. Sidnei pulled her luggage and well-packed photography equipment out of the trunk while Logan tracked down a sky hop to assist her. She looked around, people buzzing everywhere, planes coming in for landings, traffic of all sorts coming from every direction. JFK was as crazy as always. Logan had had success pretty quickly, as she saw him walking quickly back to her with sky hop in tow.

"Here you go. You tell him how you want things arranged."

She gave the sky hop directions and turned back to Logan. "It looks like I'm actually going." It was hard for Sidnei to contain her excitement. This was a trip she had wanted to make for a long time. She glowed.

"Yep. And remember, don't worry about a thing. I'll transfer your parents' money just as soon as it comes in. Zelly, Randy and crew, and Mariah all know to call me for the next several days." Sidnei thought Logan looked a little tired.

He took her by the shoulders. "And you, Sidnei Jewell, are to focus on shooting prize-winning photos of the northern lights. Period. Ready to go?"

"Yes! I'm very ready!" She hugged Logan.

"In four days, I'll be back here to pick you up."

"I hope your business meetings here in the city go well." She got on her tiptoes to kiss Logan.

"Looks like your guy is waiting for you."

Sidnei kissed Logan again and then locked her arms around him. When she stood back, Logan kissed her and turned her around. Sidnei was on her way.

It was a relatively short flight to Keflavik, though Sidnei did have time to go over her notes, make a few new ones, and enjoy a glass of wine. Once there, she gathered all her things and joined several others on a two-hour shuttle ride to Hotel Ranga, said to be a great place to view the northern lights. Situated in a rural area, Sidnei could quickly see light pollution would not be an issue. She took a big gulp of the crisp Icelandic air as she enjoyed the wild and extraordinary view from outside her suite. A river ran through the property, which was surrounded by acres of prime hiking. Sidnei laced up her hiking boots, pulled on her parka, and was off. She returned in time for the lecture on the history, science, and myth of the aurora borealis. Afterward, she ate a luscious meal of local salmon and enjoyed the comfort of her elegant but relaxed country surroundings.

Later, after the dark sky had settled in, she found herself outside stargazing with fellow photographers and astronomers. She had been anticipating the promise of a black, clear sky in this area for months. The stars were out in full force this evening, and her date with the universe for tonight was off to a good start. When she returned to her suite, Sidnei had much to share with Logan. She had him on the phone before she even closed her door.

"Hi! You won't believe what I saw this evening. The telescopes here are amazing! I saw Jupiter, the rings of Saturn, Mars, and although distant, I did get a good look at Uranus and Neptune." Sidnei spoke rapidly while pulling off her hat, coat, and gloves.

"Hey! Slow down. Good flight?"

"Oh yes, yes."

"How's the hotel?"

"Relaxing and quite elegant at the same time. Did you realize the telescopes are right here at the hotel?"

"Fantastic! Did you get some good shots?"

"It was easy."

"Northern lights?"

"Probably later this evening. How are your meetings?" Sidnei stood in the exterior doorway to her suite, taking in the night sky.

"Fine. It's good to hear you excited."

"I know! It's good to be excited."

"Nothing from Phoenix."

"I didn't expect anything. It's about time to bundle up. You wouldn't believe how dark the sky is here. Keep your fingers crossed for me."

"I will. I can't wait for your report tomorrow. Love you."

"Love you too."

Sidnei looked at her phone. Her thoughts raced as she contemplated the success of her day versus the unfathomable tragedy in Phoenix. She had to admit she was pulled to the situation in Phoenix but not so much that she could let it interfere with her life. Sidnei shook her head. She had always done her own thing, and that was just what she was going to do now. Armed with a solid carbon fiber tripod and her favorite camera, she walked out to see what this dark sky could bring her.

Once outside, she made sure her tripod was in a sturdy position, opened her camera to its widest aperture, set the camera's ISO to about 1600, and prepared to shoot an exposure of ten to fifteen seconds. She was set. Sidnei pulled up a chair and prepared to wait.

As she sat, a voice, an unwelcome voice, entered her head.

"You call that work," said her dad.

"Yes, Dad, I do. I'm a professional freelance photographer, and I'm quite good at it." Sidnei found herself squirming in her seat.

"Humph! And where's your office?"

"The world, the universe."

"Lot of craziness, just running around taking pictures, calling that a job. You should be at home with some kids."

"Not for me, Dad. That's not for me."

Sidnei shook her head. Her dad would never understand that the stars were her kids. She looked directly up at those stars. In her peripheral vision, she saw white flares shooting up from the horizon. Others saw it too and in hushed voices said to one another, "Look there! And there! Do you see it?"

The night's show had arrived. Slowly, multiple layers of white ribbons were added between the flares until the sky was filled. The flares now had faint purple fringe forming near the bottom, which were visible to the naked eye. Sidnei looked at her first camera exposures. She could not stifle her glee as she looked at her first photographs. Brilliant greens and deep purples were caught in the magnificent night sky. For the next couple of hours, she shot multiple photographs at varying focal distances.

At the end, Sidnei peered at the now dark sky and said, "Not bad for a night's work. So there, Dad!" She smiled as she packed up her equipment and walked back to her room. She slept well.

The next morning, she went for a long hike in the surrounding fields, snapping breathtaking vistas with her iPhone. The cloud formations alone were amazing. Off in the distance, snow had capped a volcano. "Ahhh ..." spilled from Sidnei's lips. She knew Logan was in meetings, but she called and left him a message. "I'm coming back here with you. It's too stunning not to share."

When she returned to the hotel, Sidnei went to the registration desk to check out activities. The horseback riding in South Iceland caught her attention immediately. Reservations were procured for the next day. This left her with a free afternoon.

Sidnei grabbed her laptop and went off to the lounge. A glass of white wine sat on the table beside her laptop. She knew she probably shouldn't, but she was going to anyway. It seemed to her that Aiden and Tam should know what was going on. She had the time this afternoon, so she was going to look for them. Aiden was easy to find. He was on LinkedIn. She made a note of his email address and moved on to look for Tam. This led from one dead end to another. So, she was back to Aiden. Taking a slow sip of wine, she asked herself, "How to start? How to start?" Sidnei drummed her fingers on the keyboard. There had never been any love lost between her and Aiden. Probably best to be straightforward. Sidnei took a deep breath and let it out slowly. *Here goes ...*

> Aiden,
> I am reaching out to let you know that Mom and Dad are not doing well, physically and financially. They need help, but as you might imagine, are resistant to whatever I offer. Resources for aging adults seem to be frozen or denied. I am hoping you might be able to lend some assistance. While Garvan is in the picture, he is a negative force. I have been unable to locate Tam. Do you have any contact numbers for him? I think we all need to work together on this.
> Sidnei

She read it over and then sent it. The next hour, she spent trying to relax in one of the resort's hot tubs, a glass of white wine in her hand. When she returned to her suite, she had a message waiting. Sidnei covered her mouth as she read, her eyes wide open.

Sidnei,

Let me first make clear this is a one-time-only contact. You will not contact me again, nor will you be able to.

I had thought you abandoned our parents years ago. They must be desperate if you are even in the picture. I will be perfectly clear. I will have nothing to do with them. When Dad asked me to go into business with him years ago, I had no idea how sinister life could be for some people. I will leave it at that. Tam discovered the same thing. He ran too. I tracked him down twenty years ago in Alaska. He was working with a fishing crew. He made it very clear he wanted no contact then or ever. So, we're both out. As for Garvan, he's a bad person. I wouldn't get involved with anything he is part of.

I always envied you growing up. You could do whatever you wanted. When you left with Logan, I thought you were the luckiest person on earth. Tam and I were left to continue to be groomed to meet Dad's expectations. So, this communique does surprise me. If I were you, I would drop whatever this is and run. They've always been desperate, and frankly, no good.

As an aside, I do run across your pictures from time to time. They're good. I also see you have continued with your horseback riding. You've made a life for yourself. You don't want to reenter theirs.

Again, do not attempt to contact me in the future. I want no part of anything related to our parents, and especially anything related to Garvan.

Aiden

Sidnei sat stunned, her mouth wide open, her heart racing. A few tears trickled down her cheeks. She swiped at the tears with the back of her hand. As she reached for her glass of wine, she slowly closed her eyes for a moment. Sinister? Desperate? No good? Aiden, Tam, and Garvan had been the focus of her parents' attention. What was he talking about? Looking at her watch, she knew Logan would probably be available now. She waited as the phone rang—once, twice. Logan answered. Sidnei spoke rapidly.

"Logan, I had some extra time today, so I thought I would try to reach

Aiden. I know I probably shouldn't have, but I sent him an email." Sidnei was swatting at her tears.

"Okay, okay. First, tell me what you sent."

Sidnei read the email she had sent to Aiden. She spoke slowly now, looking for anything that may have antagonized Aiden.

"Okay. Now read his response."

Sidnei choked on the word sinister but read on to the end. "What does he mean—*sinister*?"

"I don't know."

"He's just walking away, abandoning them."

"He may be right."

"No, I can't do that. I figured out a long time ago that they gave me something better than their love. They gave me independence. Crazy, I know. But I can't just leave them."

"Okay, Sidnei. Here's what you're going to do. You're going to put this out of your head for a few more days. Those pictures you sent me last night are fantastic! You need to focus on your pictures and relax a little."

"I know, I know, I know. Once I'm at work tonight, I'll be all right."

"Promise?"

"Promise!" Sidnei blew a noisy kiss into the phone and ended the call. She had pictures to review and notes to make, and she had promised to get to work.

After she set her camera that night, the show was almost instantaneous. The initial flares were no less spectacular as they shot up into the sky like fireworks. The ribbons ruffled the sky between the flares, as if the angels themselves were whitewashing the sky with their feathered wings and silken skirts. Sidnei took a peek at what her camera was collecting. The sky dripped in swatches of greens, blues, and purples, emeralds, sapphires, and amethysts. Clouds began to gather, adding an ethereal quality to what she saw with her naked eye and with her camera's eye. She could not contain her awe as she looked up at the sky. Last night was special; this was spectacular.

The next morning, Sidnei woke up energized and ready to ride. When the shuttle pulled up to the horse farm, she was struck by the small size of the horses grazing in the fields, their sturdy build, and their heavy coats. The owner came out to greet her, informing her she would have their best horses to choose from.

She chose a gray horse with blue eyes for her ride. She found the horse well adapted to riding, even with its short legs, for the legs were strong, the bones relatively long, and the shoulders muscular. Her horse turned out to be friendly and easy to handle, yet enthusiastic and self-assured. It had been trained well. She took it through the familiar walk, trot, and canter gaits and then moved into its two additional gaits. First, the tolt, which she knew was a natural gait for an Icelandic horse. Sidnei quickly moved her blue-eyed gray from a fast tolt walk to the speed of a normal gallop. She found this pretty impressive, but when she moved into the fifth gait called the flying pace, she was amazed. The horse had to be moving close to thirty miles an hour. The pace was a two-beat lateral gait with a moment of suspension between footfalls. It did indeed feel like flying. Sidnei looked up at the sky and laughed in sheer glee as she raised her face to the heavens and shouted, "Watch me now, Dad! Watch me now!"

On the way back to the resort, Sidnei asked her driver if they could go down to the coast. Once there, she walked along the shoreline. The waves tumbled up to the beach, wild and free. Clouds were rolling in over the islands in the distance. *Such an untamed but exquisite landscape,* she thought. She smiled, pulled her parka tighter around her, and thoughtfully walked back to the shuttle. The northern lights didn't come out that night, but the clouds over South Iceland drew many ahs and worthy pictures from Sidnei.

The sky was ablaze above the clouds as the plane pushed her home the next day. When Logan picked her up at the airport that evening, Sidnei was all smiles when she said, "Let's get this done!"

16

Sidnei left the college admission fair laden with checklists, brochures, and applications. She knew she should not have attended this event, but she didn't want to draw attention to herself. Having confirmed with admission scouts at each table she approached that there was little scholarship money provided for academic excellence, she had to admit she felt let down.

Logan came running up to her, all excited. She smiled an uncertain smile at him.

"So, you're going to go on to school?"

"No. No, I just thought I'd check it out. You know, for later." Sidnei was avoiding looking directly at Logan as she watched his smile crash out of the corner of her eye.

"Seriously? What's Ms. Gershwin going to say?"

"I've made up my mind. I'm traveling first. I have to see things ..."

"Yes, I know. I was just hoping ..."

Sidnei looked away, shrugged her shoulders, and hoped Logan didn't see her tear-filled eyes. They walked to class in silence.

When Sidnei got home, she left her stack of information on the kitchen table. She got busy with homework and forgot all about it—that is, until her dad came home from work.

"Sidnei!"

She didn't like the usual grumpy sounds her dad made when she was around. This was more than grumpy. This was angry.

"Coming!" Sidnei ran to the kitchen to find her dad tossing her application information all over the kitchen. His eyes looked like white-hot embers. She backed up a few steps.

"You were told we have no money to be sending you to school." He peered at her with his eyes now slits of cold steel.

"It was an event at school, Dad. All the seniors had to go."

"Well, you didn't. I'm not wasting my money to send a girl to school."

"And why not? I'm a good student. I work hard. I—"

"Get this in your head, Sidnei. I am not paying to send you to school. You need to get married, have some kids." Spittle flew as he spoke.

"I don't want kids. I want to travel, learn about the world."

"Get it together, girl! Be responsible. Of course you want kids. If you want to travel, you better find yourself a rich man." Her dad started to walk away.

"But I am responsible. I am. I …" Sidnei's tears fell rapidly.

"Pick up this mess and make yourself presentable for dinner. It wouldn't hurt you to wear a dress for a change."

Her dad walked out of the room, his shoulders hunched, his hands tightly clenched. Sidnei looked around the room. She put everything back into a stack and carried it upstairs to her room. From her closet, she pulled a box filled with travel brochures. Under these, Sidnei placed her college stash. She would do both in time. She knew she would. And she would do herself proud. Sidnei sat down on her bed and pulled her knees up to her chin. The tears fell steadily. When she heard her mom and brothers returning home, she carefully wiped away her tears and picked out a dress to wear for dinner.

Walking into the kitchen, Sidnei took a moment to carefully look over this family. Her mom performed her duties, especially around mealtimes, like a robot. Tonight was no exception. Aiden and Tam appeared to hang on her dad's every word. Garvan fussed and squirmed. She was her class valedictorian. Did not a single one of these people care? They all talked around her, as usual. She excused herself as soon as the meal was finished and walked outside.

As always, she found herself looking up to the sky. She would explore, she would study, and most importantly, she was going to be happy. The night sky was brilliant. Twirling around the backyard under the moon and stars and planets, she laughed. The universe was to be hers. She just knew it!

17

Sitting in the doctor's office, Sidnei and Logan kept ever-ready eyes on her mom and dad. Only a couple of weeks had passed, but Sidnei was certain they had grown a little more feeble and spacey. They looked more like their old selves, however. Her mom's hair had been done, and she sported a new manicure. The toenails would have to be addressed today, but they were carefully hidden in stockings and shoes. Sidnei had made sure. Sidnei had also made sure both her parents wore new clothes for this visit, khaki slacks with striped jerseys. Still, the staring and periods of silence were painfully evident in this small space. Sidnei caught others in the waiting room sneaking peeks at her parents. Moving them from the house to the car to the destination was more laborious than Sidnei remembered from just two weeks ago, even with Logan's help. She couldn't stop asking herself what had happened to them.

Sidnei had spoken to Zelly twice in the last two weeks. In fact, Zelly had been very helpful with the completion of the pre–doctor visit paperwork. Zelly remained concerned about her parents' medications. The meds were now disappearing almost as soon as they were picked up. Even when the meds were picked up by Zelly or the caregiver, they could be gone the very next day when one of them dropped in for a visit to see how things were going. Zelly also reported that there were very few groceries in the house as well. Yet Sidnei knew the caregiver had gone out to buy groceries twice. Garvan made himself scarce when others came to see her mom and dad, but it was obvious he was never too far away. His bed was unmade and clearly had been slept in. Towels were tossed on the bathroom floor. His trail through the house could be tracked by following the smashed beer cans and crumpled Twinkies wrappers. His clothes were scattered everywhere. Things went missing. And yet her parents continued to insist that he was helping them.

Her dad's name was called. Sidnei stood up to help her dad out of his seat. He grabbed his cane and moved slowly toward the nurse. He needed help to balance when he was asked to get up on the scale and again when he got off the scale. Once in the exam room, her dad fell into the first available seat. His blood pressure reading was alarmingly high. The nurse looked him over carefully as she made some notes. Her dad just stared.

Sidnei thanked the nurse as she left the room and then turned to her dad. "Dad, anything in particular you want the doctor to check?"

"Sure do! I wanna know why I can't see, why I can't tell if I have to pee. My big toe hurts all the time. Knee hurts. I need some pain pills, Garvan says."

"Dad, I really think what you need is physical therapy," said Sidnei, hoping her voice wasn't giving away her reaction. She was certain her own blood pressure had risen at the mention of Garvan.

"Naw! All I need are some painkillers," said her dad.

The door opened, and the nurse was now joined by the doctor, a middle-aged man with salt-and-pepper hair and muddy brown eyes. "Hello, Mr. Jepson. I'm Dr. Warren." Turning to Sidnei, he added, "And this must be your daughter, Ms. Jewell. Zelly McNulty has spoken very highly of you, as she introduced the case to me." Dr. Warren shook hands with Sidnei and her dad.

"Are you a real doctor or one of those PAs?" asked her dad.

"Well, sir, I would be an MD," said Dr. Warren. "Let's just have a listen to your heart." As Dr. Warren moved the stethoscope around her dad's chest and back, he sent a little smile and a wink toward Sidnei.

"I was thinking, Dr. Warren, that what would really help my dad would be to increase his activity," said Sidnei, returning his wink.

"I agree, Ms. Jewell. How about if we have you start by walking up and down your central hallway, Mr. Jepson. Zelly has also spoken to me about this."

"I don't know, Doctor. My knee hurts all the time. I really need somethin' for the pain."

"Well, let's take a look at that knee then," said Dr. Warren thoughtfully. Following a few manipulations with her dad's knee and a quick consult with her dad's file, Dr. Warren stepped back and folded his arms across his chest. "Mr. Jepson, you do need to use this knee more. I'm going to ask Zelly to coordinate some in-home physical therapy for you. Right now, I see I need to have one of my people come in and trim your toenails. Your medications should remain the same," said Dr. Warren, as he prepared to leave.

"Dr. Warren, if I could have a few moments of your time?" asked Sidnei.

"Certainly, Ms. Jewell. Please come with me. Mr. Jepson, good day!"

A young and attractive female technician had come into the exam room and already had one of her dad's feet in her lap. Her dad was fully engaged with the technician.

Sidnei closed the door behind her and followed Dr. Warren to his office. Each took a seat on either side of the desk. Dr. Warren clasped his hands and appeared to be carefully weighing what he was about to say.

"Thank you for taking this time to talk with me," said Sidnei.

"No problem. Zelly has informed me about the vagaries of your parents' cases. Any chance they could go into assisted living?" asked Dr. Warren.

"Oh my! We haven't even broached that topic yet. They aren't very good with changes they don't orchestrate themselves since Dad retired."

"Ms. Jewell, from what I have learned and briefly seen, they really should not be on their own." He had formed a cupola with his fingers as he looked intently at Sidnei.

"I know! I know! My husband and I are concerned about their safety, but they keep dismissing the topic."

"Before they leave today, I would like you to sit in on a dementia prescreening test for each of them. I'm concerned that they're not only physically unable to be on their own but also mentally."

Sidnei held on to the arms of her chair while she made herself breathe in and out, in and out. She had to blink back the tears several times before she spoke.

"Okay, I do understand your concerns. How much do you know about my brother?" asked Sidnei.

"Enough to say I share your concern about their general well-being," said Dr. Warren.

"Neither the police nor the bank is willing to investigate," said Sidnei, openly fighting back tears.

"Sadly, I hear that often, more so lately. I will tell you that our office has initiated a request for a Medicare fraud investigation, but they often fall by the wayside. Should this request go forward, someone may contact you," said Dr. Warren.

"Thank you for that," said Sidnei, taking a deep breath and swiping at a tear escaping down her cheek.

Sidnei did a quick scan of Dr. Warren's office. It was almost bare of any personal effects. A lone picture on the counter behind his desk showed two women, one older, one younger. A wife? A daughter? Did they know what a caring man they had in their lives?

"I should get back to my dad," said Sidnei, standing.

"It was a pleasure to meet you, Ms. Jewell. I'm sorry the circumstances are not better for everyone." He rose to shake Sidnei's hand.

Sidnei walked back down the hall and knocked quietly on the exam room door.

"Please come in," a pleasant voice said.

"Sidnei, do you know why I can't have pain pills?" asked her dad gruffly.

"Dad, I told you myself that I don't think you need them."

"Why are you always trying to be so smart?" he said, staring down at the floor.

"It's a gift, Dad. One that I inherited."

The nurse looked at both of them and then said, "If I could have your attention, Mr. Jepson. I need to ask you some questions."

"Okay. Ask," said her dad.

"First of all, I'm going to say three words that you need to remember for later. Apple, piano, mirror. Okay?"

"Okay! Okay!" Her dad's irritability was evident. Even though he looked down at the floor, there was no missing his pouty mouth.

The nurse took him through the clock part of the exercise orally. Her dad did all right drawing a clock in the air and identifying where each of the numbers, one through twelve, would appear on a clock face. When asked to tell the nurse where the hands would point for 4:40, he was stymied. When asked to repeat the three words he had been asked to remember, he grew angry.

"I can get through my days just fine without remembering any such nonsense!" shouted her dad. He shut down after that.

When her mom was given a similar test about an hour later, she struggled to place the numbers in their correct places on the clock face, making it impossible for her to draw the hands pointing to the numbers to read 3:15. She did, however, remember two of her three words. Her mom looked blankly at Sidnei and then cried and hung her head.

At the end of the two appointments, Sidnei was called back into Dr. Warren's office. He gravely explained that her parents' dementia was in the medium range. Further, her mom did need pain medication, but in light of the suspicion that any narcotics prescribed might never make it to her mom, he was suggesting patches to alleviate the pain. Dr. Warren reiterated the need for assisted living, maybe even a skilled nursing facility.

Sidnei walked slowly back to the reception area. Her parents sat on either side of Logan, each with their hands clasped around their canes standing in front of them. They were ready to go. Logan was casually flipping through a magazine. Sidnei placed herself directly in front of Logan. As he looked up, Sidnei quietly said, "Let's go, please."

Sidnei assisted Logan in helping her dad to his feet. Then she moved to her mom and gave her an arm to help her stand up. The four of them lumbered out to the car.

Once all were safely secured in the car, Sidnei said, "Let's go to lunch."

"Can we go to the shrimp place again?" asked her mom.

"You betcha!" said Sidnei. She was watching her dad out of the corner of her eye. He appeared lost in thought.

"Dad, you're kind of quiet. Did the doctor's visit wear you out?"

Her dad looked up. "Sidnei, do you know why the doctor won't give me pain pills?" Sidnei thought her dad looked like he might cry.

"Dad, you don't need them. You just need to move more." While she was pointing out which direction Logan should turn, Sidnei still watched her dad.

"Humph," said her dad, now staring down at his lap.

"And here we are! Everybody better be hungry," said Sidnei.

Sidnei and Logan methodically went through the car exit routine with her parents. Restaurant staff again readily appeared to assist. Once seated and served, they all ate quietly. When the table was cleared and they were waiting for dessert, Sidnei broached the topic that was resurfacing from the recesses of her mind.

"I haven't heard much lately about Garvan's girls. What have they been up to?" Sidnei asked.

Sidnei looked at both of her parents. The new shirts had food stains on them. Both of her parents looked worn out. Her mom turned to her dad with big, frightened eyes. Her dad kept his head down. Her mom mumbled, "Oh, their mother won't let him see them."

"Goodness! Why is that?"

"We, we don't know. Garvan is such a good dad," said her mom, looking frantically for some place to focus on. Her lips were drawn in a straight line.

"Interesting," said Sidnei as she received a subtle nudge from Logan.

"Well, here's dessert!" said Sidnei. Little was said for the remainder of the meal. Her mom and dad worked on consuming their lemon meringue pie and avoided talking.

Logan looked at his watch as they were finishing up. "We better get a move on if we want to meet the lockbox people on time."

Sidnei and Logan helped her mom and dad out to the car. The drive home was quiet and quick. Her parents quickly sought refuge in their chairs and turned their attention to the TV before they fell asleep. Sidnei and Logan moved down the hall to the living room and the front door. There they waited for the firemen who would be installing the lockbox.

"Well, that was a bit awkward," said Logan.

"Yep! But then this whole situation is awkward. I just wonder what Garvan did," said Sidnei.

"Me too," said Logan. "Guess I'm not the only one he creeps out."

"Most assuredly not." Sidnei had her eye on a vehicle pulling up to the house, with Fire Department written on the side. "Looks like our people are here."

The two firemen were good-looking, middle-aged men who were very amiable. They explained that they had installed many lockboxes for the elderly over the years. It was a small metal box that they installed by the front door. One of the new house keys was put inside. As the firemen were explaining that they and the police had their own special key to open the box, Garvan appeared from out of nowhere.

"You mean you guys can get into the house any time you want?" Garvan spit the words out. His fists were knuckled, his jaw clenched. Protruding from a filthy T-shirt was a massive belly. He swayed a little and reeked of beer and pot and body odor.

"Yep, Garvan, if there's anything suspicious going on that arouses our attention," said one of the firemen.

Sidnei and Logan looked at each other, wide-eyed. Remembering her last two encounters with Garvan, Sidnei reached for Logan's hand and squeezed tight.

"You know one another?" asked Logan.

"Yes, we do," said the other fireman. Both men kept on working on the lockbox.

"Shouldn't you be at home taking care of Mom and Dad? That's what they say you do, take care of them. The house could use a good cleaning, by the way." The words tumbled from Sidnei's mouth. She knew she was probably cutting off the circulation in Logan's hand, but she stared at Garvan with her head cocked to one side.

"You, you ... That's women's work. You could be doing the cleaning when you take the time out to come and visit." Garvan was dancing from one foot to the other. His eyes looked in every direction. He arched his back and began to raise his fists.

The two firemen looked up at the two siblings. Garvan brought his fists back down. Sidnei took a deep breath.

"Jeez! You two can't leave anything alone!" Shouting profanities, Garvan stormed down the sidewalk and walked quickly around the corner and out of sight.

Sidnei gaped but shut her mouth quickly. Her whole body shook as she moved into Logan's arms.

"Don't worry, ma'am. We have eyes on this place," said both firemen.

"Thank you! Thank you!" said Sidnei.

"You'll want to talk to your parents about wearing emergency alert monitors. Those things help alert us too. Good day to both of you," said one of the firemen before they took their leave.

"Where did he come from? Remember I told you he popped up at the neighbor's house when I went looking for him a couple of weeks ago? He's like a subterranean creature. And he smells! Lord!" said Sidnei.

Logan put one hand on Sidnei's shoulder and rubbed her back with his other hand.

"He frightens me," said Sidnei.

"Me too."

"Why do my parents keep saying he takes care of them? He's doing something evil here. I just know it. Aiden was trying to say the same thing, I think."

Sidnei turned in toward Logan's chest and sobbed. "I have to get them out of here."

Logan held her tight.

"There has to be a way," Sidnei whispered. "There just has to be a way."

The late-afternoon Phoenix winds were beginning to kick up. Sidnei could smell the dust and feel the dirt and grit slapping at her skin.

18

Sitting in Ms. Gershwin's office, Sidnei waited politely for the guidance counselor to return. Sidnei smoothed her navy blue mini-skirt over her lap. She twisted a few of her blonde curls. Pretty certain that she knew why Ms. Gershwin had called her to the guidance office, Sidnei began to tap her feet. She really wanted to get this over with.

Breezing into the office, Ms. Gershwin gushed, "Oh my! You always look so pretty, Sidnei!"

"Thank you, Ms. Gershwin," said Sidnei.

"Now, Sidnei, I was looking through your file, and I don't see any college applications waiting to be processed. You see, deadlines are fast approaching," said Ms. Gershwin as she flipped back and forth through the paperwork in front of her.

"Ms. Gershwin, I will not be attending college," said Sidnei.

Ms. Gershwin looked up from the paperwork and stared at Sidnei. "But of course you are. You have such a beautiful mind."

"No, ma'am, I am not able to go. Right after graduation, I will be going on an extensive backpacking trip," said Sidnei, keeping her focus. She didn't dare lose this focus, for she knew it was what was keeping her from breaking into tears.

"Oh well, surely you'll be back in the fall to begin your first semester," said Ms. Gershwin.

"No, ma'am ..."

"I'm going to have a talk with your parents," said Ms. Gershwin before Sidnei could continue.

"I wish you wouldn't. The decision was made long ago. I'll be fine, my dad says." Sidnei stood. She held out her hand to shake, but Ms. Gershwin grabbed it with both of her hands.

"Sidnei, I don't know what to say." Ms. Gershwin's eyes filled with tears. "You're at the top of your class, and you ... you're such a promising student."

"I really will be fine. I always am," said Sidnei. She turned and retreated down the hall. She had to push aside a brief flashback to her dad's anger when she brought home the college fair information. She would not dwell on it; she would not give him the satisfaction. Tossing her curls, Sidnei picked up her pace as she headed for her physics class.

Once in the classroom, Sidnei settled in quickly. This was an environment where she was comfortable, a place where she could not only share her ideas but also receive accolades for them. She would continue with school after graduation; Sidnei knew this for sure. She just wasn't sure when that would happen. Right now, she wanted to pursue the rocket launch project before her. Sidnei gave her curls an especially good toss and got to work.

Later in the day, Sidnei picked up Tam from school and dropped him off at ball practice. This gave her an hour to enjoy an espresso and to work on her homework. Pulling into a parking spot right in front of the coffee shop, she did a quick double take. The couple sitting at the table by the window was strangely familiar. Yet that couldn't be her dad. He didn't even drink coffee. She couldn't actually see the man's face. The young woman she had seen before a while back, but where? The attractive woman had wavy red hair and was probably in her early twenties. Sidnei just couldn't place her, but the two people looked really wrong. Sidnei could not make herself move out of the car. She slowly backed out of the parking space and drove to the library. She convinced herself she had been mistaken and immersed herself in conjugating French verbs.

That evening, when her family gathered for dinner, her dad, as usual, carried on an animated conversation with her brothers. If it had been him at the coffee shop, wouldn't he have recognized her car? And wouldn't he say something about it now? Sidnei quickly convinced herself that she had been mistaken. Nothing was said about a phone call from Ms. Gershwin either, so Sidnei considered herself good on all fronts. Though she still thought she had seen the young woman in the coffee shop window before.

19

Garvan, or rather the "phantom extortionist," as Sidnei and Logan were now referring to him, must have hightailed it to the bank after the altercation at the front door with Sidnei, Logan, and the firemen. A thousand dollars had been pulled out of an ATM machine later that same day in three transactions, resulting in an extra hundred dollars charged in overdraft fees. The bank would not relent on their policy. The police would not agree to speak to her parents, whom they insisted would assure them they had given permission for the withdrawals.

Finding more roadblocks than open pathways in Phoenix, Sidnei and Logan made an appointment with their private attorney in Pennsylvania. They now sat in the attorney's conference room, relaying to him all the recent events. The room was tastefully appointed in muted blues and browns. Sidnei had found the room calming previously, but today she found it less so. In fact, Sidnei was exhausted after rehashing all the disturbing findings and events swirling around her parents' situation.

The attorney paused in his notetaking. He spoke slowly and thoughtfully.

"You could petition Garvan for an accounting of the trust you mentioned on the phone. He sounds like he could be held accountable for producing such an accounting since he has been identified by your parents as the one in charge," said the attorney.

"He doesn't pay any of their bills though. He doesn't even take them to the doctor." Sidnei looked down at her lap as she said this. The retelling was truly depressing. When she looked up, she could not dismiss the perplexity on the attorney's face.

"Then, am I to assume the two of you are paying the bills?" The attorney now looked squarely at both of them.

"Yes, and paying the caregiving company, the restaurant that delivers their meals, the copay for their doctor visits and lab work ..." Sidnei shook her head and sighed.

"And don't forget the new air conditioner," said Logan.

The attorney now shook his head. "You really do need to get your parents to sign a promissory note for the mortgage payments and all the other expenses you're incurring."

"Okay. We can work on that," said Sidnei.

"You also need to look into redoing the trust with Sidnei's name on it," said the attorney.

"There may be no money for securing a new trust. Phoenix home prices for the most part are all underwater. Homes are worth far less right now than their mortgages. And, as near as we can tell, there's no savings left," Sidnei explained.

"Life insurance?" The attorney looked at Sidnei, then Logan.

"Don't know," said Logan.

"My fear is that there's no life insurance, but we'll look into it," said Sidnei. She could feel her heart trying to stab out beats. This was more and more frightening.

"One more thought. I recommend you get Adult Protective Services involved since the bank and the police are reluctant to pursue any kind of investigation."

Sidnei looked at Logan. "Wow," she said quietly. "Wow. Dad will go through the roof. But what else can we do? The doctor and Zelly have expressed their concerns. This sounds like the next step," said Sidnei. She looked intently at Logan.

"I agree it needs to be pursued," said Logan. He reached for Sidnei's hand.

"This will bring everything to a whole new level," said Sidnei. She closed her eyes and took a deep breath, giving Logan's hand a squeeze.

The attorney's secretary came in to say the attorney from Phoenix was on the line. Sidnei and Logan's attorney brought the new attorney up to date with what they were encountering. To everything that the three of them had discussed, the Phoenix attorney added that they should consider a corporate conservatorship.

Sidnei's head was spinning. Each issue just led to more issues. Sidnei was getting a little nauseous as more legalese was taking over the conversation. That old knot in the pit of her stomach was tightening. This was all so new and unfamiliar, like all those schools she had attended as a child. She signaled to bring the conversation to a close. Both attorneys were thanked, and Sidnei and Logan were on their way.

"Whew! This is bigger than I want to believe," said Sidnei, collapsing into the passenger seat of their car and cradling her head in her hands.

"I know. Makes my parents' unfortunate accidental deaths, and the aftermath so long ago, seem relatively straightforward," said Logan as he pulled into traffic.

"Do you think Garvan would respond to an accounting request?" asked Sidnei, staring out the car window.

"No way! I do like the promissory note idea for legal purposes, though I don't have any hope anything will be repaid," said Logan.

"I know. I'm sorry, Logan, but I can't let them be homeless. I really think we need to look into assisted living options for them. I've been giving it a lot of thought," said Sidnei.

"Sidnei, I don't want you worrying about the money. We can afford to do this until we find more realistic alternatives for your parents," said Logan.

"Thanks. There's such a big disconnect between my parents and me. I don't always know what to do."

"I hear you. We'll just keep moving ahead. What do you think about contacting APS?" asked Logan.

"I have to say I think it's a next step even though it may rattle my parents, and probably more so Garvan. Honestly, I think it's a little scary. But I'm going to do it," said Sidnei with conviction.

Sidnei and Logan pulled into their driveway and exited their car, meeting at the back door where they hugged a long, long time.

Pulling apart, Logan said, "I love you, Sidnei." He looked at her longingly, lovingly.

"But I love you more!" said Sidnei, holding both of her hands over her heart.

The air had a slight chill. The leaves were turning gold, orange, and red and swirled around their feet. The season was changing rapidly now. As Sidnei looked tenderly at Logan, she wondered just how many more changes lay ahead for them. She gave Logan a quick kiss as she reached for his hand. United, they held hands as they walked through the door.

20

Sidnei gazed in the mirror as she carefully brushed her blonde curls. They fell in gently flowing waves nearly to her waist. Her white silk sheath shimmered in the late-afternoon light coming in through her bedroom window. That familiar radiance surrounded her. She had grown accustomed to it and felt comforted by its sheltering presence at this moment. Sidnei was happy to be graduating, happy to be moving into true independence away from her family. She would leave tomorrow to backpack through the Rockies with Logan and several of her closest friends. They had hired guides and horses. Truly a dream, an idea long in the making, now come true.

Sidnei sighed and smiled as she turned to look at the gown hanging behind her. It had a simple, rounded neckline, gathered at the waist, and fanned out to reveal white peau de soie roses outlined in pearls cascading to the floor. She remembered her dad's look of astonishment when Logan had asked for his permission to marry Sidnei. Her dad had looked at each of them and then shook his head saying, "Take good care of her," as he walked away. Her mom had nothing to say when Sidnei showed her the sparkling engagement ring. She just smiled that fake smile of hers with her lips held in a straight line, blinked, and then turned and walked away.

A few days later, Sidnei's dad gave her an envelope. Inside the envelope were ten crisp hundred-dollar bills along with a list of three hundred names.

"Sidnei, these are the people you are to invite. You can have the party at our house. I already checked with Father McCall, and your date is set at the church. Your mom and I will feed the people. This money needs to cover your dress, flowers, cake, photographer, and any other nonsense you might want."

"Thanks, Dad," said Sidnei. The money felt heavy somehow.

"This Logan, he's smart I hear. I know that means something to you. I sure hope he uses those smarts to make some money," said her dad as he prepared to leave the room. "Good luck," he added as he walked out.

Sidnei shopped secondhand shops and bargain basements for months. Then one day, she saw this dress, now her dress, added to a window display. A friend's mom altered it for her. It was perfect! And it made her feel pretty. Sidnei was to borrow a veil from one of her cousins. Logan said he had a surprise coming for her bouquet. She and her friends would do fresh flowers for the altar the morning of the ceremony. The local Shop N Bag would do the cake with only a few days' notice. A good friend would take the pictures, and several others would do the music. Her whole family would attend the wedding, the one event where they would watch her rather than her watching them.

She would still have some of her dad's wedding cash left over. This small sum she would use to help with setting up the apartment she and Logan would move into following the wedding. Logan had received a full scholarship covering tuition, books, family housing rent, and a small monthly stipend. Sidnei would work at a nationally recognized horse farm helping with horseback riding lessons and competitions. There would be enough extra money each month that she had already registered for one class at a nearby community college.

Sidnei pulled her shoulders back and smiled. Her great adventure would begin tomorrow at sunrise. Tonight there was high school graduation, where Sidnei would deliver the senior farewell speech. She would speak of the importance of dreams and their realization, of reaching for the moon and beyond.

Her mother was calling her. Sidnei took one last measure of herself in the mirror and winked. She could truly say she liked this person named Sidnei. This evening marked a major new beginning for her. Sidnei beamed as she slowly descended the steps.

The evening began filled with good wishes. In fact, her mom actually smiled a real smile and wiped away a few tears when Sidnei walked across the stage to receive her diploma. Her dad had explained that he had business meetings for this evening and could not attend. Sidnei spied him at the back of the auditorium in the doorway when she delivered her speech. Now, as she completed her walk across the stage, she once again found him at the rear of the auditorium. Only now, there was someone with him, a familiar face, this time young, athletic, blonde, but from where? Sidnei's heart stopped for a brief moment as she struggled to keep smiling. This was not the young woman from the coffee shop but another young woman on her father's arm. This young woman Sidnei remembered as a cheerleader from one of the high schools where her father had taught and coached. As a cheerleader, the woman had followed her father around, fawning and preening, and well, what? The two of them had vanished in the crowd. Sidnei returned to her seat beside Logan, reached for Logan's hand, gave it a squeeze, and retreated to her happy place for a while.

The next morning, Sidnei carried her gear out to the van and didn't look back. She returned the day before her wedding, radiated happiness at the ceremony, changed clothes at her home before she and Logan went off to begin their lives, and was aware that no one but their backpacking friends noticed when she and Logan left. The day was autumn crisp and promised changes to come.

21

Back home in Pennsylvania, elbows propped on the table, Sidnei rested her head on her hands as she looked at the array of brochures and information placed before her. Over a two-month span, she and Logan had visited twenty assisted living places in Pennsylvania. Now, Sidnei sorted through the information they had collected.

Sidnei and Logan had agreed that her parents' own income had to support this living arrangement. That meant that right away Sidnei could eliminate several, as they were too expensive. Then there were a few geared toward retired university professors. Her parents would not be comfortable in those environments. Like Logan and herself, those professors were eggheads, heads in the clouds, impractical. She could hear her dad's litany against the sins of what he generally referred to as the overeducated. A few other assisted living establishments were merely places where people went to sit until they died. The people in those places neither spoke nor made eye contact. They looked tired and sad. That left two possibilities. Each was comfortable, homey, well staffed, and appeared to genuinely like the elderly. Sidnei was so excited that she uncharacteristically reached for the phone and called her parents' number.

Surprisingly, her mom answered, "Hello," a tentative, almost frightened hello. Sidnei immediately realized she might be treading in insecure waters since she had not strategized how to sell her parents on the assisted living option.

"Hey, Mom! I have some great news for you!" Sidnei barreled ahead.

"Well, that's nice, Sidnei. What is it?" asked her mom, still sounding a little hesitant.

"Logan and I have been looking into assisted living places here for you and Dad. I think we found a couple you'll like."

"Sidnei, we're not moving. We're just not up to it. Besides, I don't want to leave my home. And where would Garvan go?"

Sidnei's mind reeled. Garvan, always Garvan. She could feel herself tensing up, making fists, and tapping her feet.

Taking a deep breath before she responded, Sidnei spoke carefully. "Mom, you and Dad need a lot of assistance. Garvan isn't there very often. I worry about you and Dad being alone."

"Oh my, we're not alone. You have those people coming by, Sidnei. We're fine. We're really just fine," said her mom. "Here's your dad."

"Sidnei, I want to talk to you about the meals. They're pretty skimpy, and ..."

Sidnei could hear her mom interrupting in the background, "Gabe, the meals are just fine. Sidnei wants us to move, and I'm not moving again. Don't go giving her reasons for us to move."

"What? I'll take care of this," said her dad as he returned to talk to Sidnei. "Sidnei, we aren't moving, and that's final!" Her dad hung up.

Sidnei set her phone down. She grabbed a sweater hanging by the back door and walked for miles as she went over the phone call, including how it went and how it should have gone. When she returned home, Sidnei made careful notes before she called Adult Protective Services.

Sidnei had called APS weeks ago with her concerns. APS had, in turn, explained that they were backlogged with their investigations. Sidnei could not wait any longer. Her call was transferred to her parents' caseworker. This, she hoped, was a good sign.

"Hello. Terry, here. How may I help you?" asked a voice that sounded neither young nor old.

"I'm Sidnei Jewell, the daughter of Gabe and Jezzi Jepson."

"Oh sure. I visited your parents yesterday and was working on my report just now. Typically, though, we don't talk to the family members when we don't see any signs of abuse," said Terry.

"What? There's missing medication, missing food. The house is filthy, and much of it we found in disrepair. Doctors are reluctant to see my parents because they suspect my brother is selling their medications. They're totally isolated from others. They don't look or act like themselves," said Sidnei, the words tumbling out.

"Well, ma'am, I found no evidence of abuse. Your brother Garvan was there, and he was very helpful in correcting the positioning of your mom's knee when it was making her uncomfortable. I'm guessing your parents are abusing their meds themselves and probably need pain management assistance, though they deny it. In fact, they denied everything," said Terry. His voice sounded disinterested, preoccupied.

"What! Garvan is the abuser! He takes everything they've ever had—drugs, groceries, cars, their dignity. He periodically wipes out their bank account, leaving them nothing!"

Terry heatedly interrupted, "All you siblings are all alike. You need to understand that he provides twenty-four-hour care, so any monies he's consumed are actually earned. Families often think this is unfair, but in Garvan's case, he's providing care."

"He is not! He should be overseeing their medications and making sure there's money each month for them to pay their bills and put groceries on the table. Instead, he takes everything. And I do mean *everything!*"

"And how do you know your parents didn't choose to use their resources differently? The bottom line is their decisions, their choices. They indicated they are perfectly happy with the way things are," said Terry, undeniably angry.

"They're both suffering from dementia," said Sidnei. A quiet despair was evident in her voice.

"My report will show that I didn't see any evidence they are unable to care for themselves, with a little of Garvan's help. I might add that there are a lot of old people who like to get high," said Terry, with a sinister laugh at the end.

"I thought you were supposed to protect the elderly," Sidnei said before she hung up. She stood up with clenched fists. Then she reached for the notebook where she kept a record of all the interactions concerning her parents. She threw it across the room, scattering papers and brochures. Sidnei raised her head and screamed a primal scream. She slung herself across the room, out the door, and walked and cried, and walked and cried. Slowing down after a while, she dried her tears and sat to collect her thoughts. Concluding there was evil afoot in Phoenix, she rose and made her way home.

Carefully she gathered up her notes. Setting them aside, she went to her studio and put the final finishing touches on her Iceland articles. One was on the northern lights, the other on the Icelandic horse, and both were beautifully illustrated with her photos. The work soothed her and kept her focused. Work was always an elixir for her.

When Logan returned home that evening, Sidnei relayed the whole conversation with the APS worker word for word. Logan looked painfully incredulous throughout the account. Sidnei finished up by saying, "Logan, 'their choices, their decisions' is, in my opinion, nothing more than jargon for the authorities to dismiss their responsibilities to the elderly. I don't know where else to turn." Sidnei started crying again as Logan put his arms around her.

"Sidnei, this isn't fair. It's not even moral. You're right about it being evil. The bottom line for me is twofold. We need to get them out of that house, and we need to better secure their money. Let's start with the money issue while we think about how to get them to move."

The moon had come out while Sidnei and Logan spoke. It offered light over the dark night.

22

Sidnei and Logan not only never looked back, but they also pushed ahead building very successful lives. Asked to be an assistant equestrian coach for the Olympics, Sidnei gained early notoriety. Her dad kept asking, how was riding a damn horse a sport? Sidnei ignored the question. Logan doggedly pursued a PhD in chemical engineering, worked hard at this passion of his, and now had his own consulting firm. Her dad always wanted to know if Logan made any real money doing this kind of thing. Logan ignored the question. Sidnei took classes steadily over the years and ended up with a double major in astronomy and creative writing. She worked as a freelance writer, submitting articles on where the sun, moon, planets, stars, and constellations were in relation to each of the places she traveled to. This made it possible for her to do her work wherever she might be on the planet. This also allowed her a great deal of flexibility, which her dad said was like having no job, at best an indulgence. Sidnei laughed and wandered further and further away from her parents.

Her parents kept moving all over the United States once Garvan graduated from high school. Sidnei and Logan visited increasingly less frequently. Her dad grew ever more caustic. Her mom became more distracted and out of touch with the world at large. When Sidnei and Logan went to visit after her parents moved to Phoenix, they were met at the front door by an angry dad.

"Humph! You two slumming? All those fancy trips of yours … hardly ever coming around here. C'mon in. I want to talk to you, Sidnei," said her dad.

Sidnei and Logan, eyebrows raised, made it down the long hall to the family room. There her mom met them with a hug and a kiss for each of them.

"Sit down, Sidnei. You know it might be nice if you sent your mom more practical gifts, like money to get her hair done or her nails." Her dad paused as he seethed with anger.

Sidnei looked in her mom's direction. She appeared perfect in every way. Her hair had been cut and colored, fingers and toes were done in fun colors. She wore a pair of stylish slacks with a color-coordinated tunic. And she smelled like roses and lilacs. Yep, that was her mom looking like a million dollars!

"Sidnei, pay attention! That's been your problem your whole life. Your attention is always someplace else. Those flowers aren't what your mother needs," said her dad.

"Now, Gabe, what are you doing?" Her mom looked puzzled and worried.

"You stay out of this, Jezzi! Sidnei acts like she isn't even part of this family. Next time you decide to come, bring your mom some money!" Her dad picked up the flowers, holding them over Sidnei's head. "Not any damn flowers!"

"That's enough, Gabe. We should go, Sidnei," said Logan as he pulled out Sidnei's chair. He took Sidnei's arm as she stood, and the two of them exited the house quickly.

Her mom could be heard in the distance wailing, "What have you done? What have you done?"

Unmistakably, Garvan's laughter could also be heard in the distance as Sidnei and Logan left the house. Yet neither of them could remember seeing him in the house.

23

Sidnei came dashing into their Pennsylvania bank. Logan had called to say he had an appointment with the bank manager at four to discuss setting up a new account for her parents. She didn't see Logan in the lobby, so she took a seat. Her ears immediately pricked up as the person in the office to her right engaged in an angry conversation. She bent a little to her right.

"Yeah, I went over to Mom's. There's hardly anything there. Mom says she doesn't know where it all went. She was mostly upset though about her money. It's gone. It's all gone. I thought Candice agreed to take care of Mom, but she's nowhere to be found. Mom says she hasn't seen her in weeks."

Sidnei sat back and sighed. She had always known it wasn't just her parents. Sadly, it was good, well, not really good, but reassuring to hear others were dealing with similar situations. But why did the elderly have to deal with this? What about the elderly who had no one to turn to? It made her ill. Logan arrived, and they were ushered into an office across the reception area. Without going too deeply into the painful details, Sidnei and Logan outlined how and why they were here today. Though trying to show no emotion, the bank manager winced toward the end of the bare-bones description of the nightmare they had walked into. This was followed by a thoughtful silence.

"I believe we can help you. You said their monthly stipends are automatically deposited each month, correct?"

"That's correct," said Logan. Sidnei nodded her assent.

"We can set up an account here for your parents with your names on the account. You'll have to reroute their deposits. However, you, Ms. Jewell, will have to have financial power of attorney," said the bank manager, looking intently at Sidnei.

"Okay. Can that be done here in Pennsylvania?" asked Sidnei.

"It should be done in the state where your parents reside. It sounds like that is not likely to be Pennsylvania," said the bank manager.

Sidnei could hear the clock on the bank manager's desk tick off each passing second. She closed her eyes, took a deep breath, and said, "All right. I guess we know what we have to do."

"Just one more thing. You might want to make an appointment with Social Security. They will likely want you to consider becoming your parents' representative payee. That will require opening a second account. It's a nifty little program that deposits their checks into an account in your name, giving you direct control over the money and how it is spent. Could be helpful," said the bank manager.

Sidnei and Logan thanked the bank manager, shook his hand, and exited the bank, promising to return soon.

Once in the car, Logan turned to Sidnei and asked, "So where do you think they would agree to move to?"

"We know PA is out of the question for them. They've lived all over the US but chose Phoenix for retirement. Almost everyone there has put up roadblocks, so Arizona is out of the question for me," said Sidnei.

"I agree. But where?" Logan asked.

"Well, that's the million-dollar question," said Sidnei. "I've been thinking about this a lot though. They met in Colorado, so why not look there?"

"You mean that little town, Weston, Watson, Weldon …" said Logan.

"Watkins, yes, I do mean Watkins," said Sidnei.

"I don't know, Sidnei. There's never been much there. Would there even be an assisted living place out there?"

"I'm going to look into it. There are so many farms and cattle ranches around that I can't imagine most of the residents wouldn't want their elderly members at least nearby," said Sidnei, pulling up Watkins on her computer.

"You honestly think they would want to go there? They've become pretty much big-city people over the years," said Logan.

"I'm very sure. I was looking through some more of their paperwork we brought home and verified that I remembered correctly that they have burial plots there," said Sidnei, putting up her hand for a high five.

Logan exchanged a high five with her, shaking his head and smiling. "That's my Sidnei!"

As Logan broke away, he said, "I thought your mom wouldn't move out of her house."

"Well, we're going to have to convince her otherwise. Remember, Dr. Warren said they both need this kind of setting. Zelly did too. Maybe they can help us," said Sidnei.

"Okay. I guess a plan is starting to take shape. Let's make sure we have all of our facts, concerns, and reasons in a package before we share our thoughts with your parents, though," said Logan.

"Oh, I've learned my lesson. This time, I will indeed come prepared with facts, statistics, and well-researched reasons," said Sidnei, a bright glimmer in her blue eyes.

Over the next weeks, Sidnei and Logan returned to Phoenix to check on her parents and to restock their steadily vanishing food and supplies. Logan joked that maybe Garvan had a family nearby. Sidnei did not laugh.

During this trip, they met with Dr. Warren and with Zelly to share their plan and to get valuable information concerning Sidnei's parents that would be relevant to their plan. Both Dr. Warren and Zelly implored them to move as quickly as they could and to look at skilled nursing facilities with progressive dementia care. Dr. Warren expressed concerns that he thought their dementia was accelerating at an alarming rate.

Sidnei and Logan also met with a real estate agent while they were in Phoenix. From this meeting, they learned three key pieces of information. First, in Sidnei's parents' neighborhood, almost every home was "underwater," meaning the owners had borrowed against their mortgage, and the owners now had a mortgage greater than the worth of the house. This was most definitely true for Sidnei's parents. While this did not surprise Sidnei and Logan, it further raised the question about where all the money was going. Second, there were programs to work with homes that were underwater that allowed the banks to sell these homes. Third, Arizona had a law in place that would name Sidnei the power of attorney, specifically to sell the house. While not all good news, it did offer help and hope.

On their final day in Phoenix, Sidnei and Logan went to check in with her parents once more before they caught their plane. Garvan suddenly appeared. He entered the house, making a growling sound as he made his way to his bedroom. He slammed his bedroom door and screamed, "Get her and that deadbeat out of here!"

Sidnei marched to his bedroom door and threw it open.

"Why don't you say that directly to me, Garvan?" She stood tall and worked to keep her voice even.

"Get out!" Garvan roared.

"Actually, I think it's you who needs to get out. You're killing our parents. I don't know exactly how you're getting away with this, but I'm working on it."

Garvan moved a step forward.

Sidnei raised her chin to look directly into Garvan's eyes.

"You know, I just realized that you don't intimidate me. You're just a bully. And again, it's you who needs to leave."

Garvan brushed past her and ran out the door cursing.

Sidnei swallowed, took a breath, and walked back to her parents. She hoped no one would notice she was shaking.

Her mom quietly said, "Oh, don't mind him. He's havin' a bad day."

"He seems to have a lot of those, Mom. I find his perpetual foul mood frightening," said Sidnei, wrapping her arms around her waist.

"Naw, Sidnei. That's just the way he is. Let it alone," said her dad dully, staring straight ahead.

Sidnei opened her mouth to reply, but before she could say anything, Logan had her by the arm. He suggested it was time for them to leave.

"Oh my gosh! You're right! We should be heading to the airport," said Sidnei, hugging her mom and blowing a noisy kiss toward her dad.

"See you soon!" And Sidnei and Logan were on their way again.

Once in the car, Logan reached over to give Sidnei a hug and said, "Maybe it's best if you don't try to be the tough cop."

"I know, but I can't stand being told over and over again that there's nothing that can be done. He's evil, and he must be stopped. Besides, facing up to him just now felt good."

"I don't trust him, just like I wouldn't trust an ax murderer. Please try to keep a little distance."

Sidnei smiled. "Okay, but I'm still going to confront him when I see him. A Garvan sighting doesn't happen often."

"Okay, okay. But tread lightly. Now back home."

Regrouped and refocused once back home in Pennsylvania, Sidnei and Logan continued their research. Discovering that there were over ninety skilled nursing facilities within about thirty miles of Watkins, Sidnei decided to call all those on the list within fifteen miles. She was able to narrow the list quickly to five that had dedicated dementia units within their facilities.

Sidnei's first phone call to the skilled nursing facility at the top of her list was a little disconcerting. She explained the situation to the director, who, in turn, asked an unexpected question.

"Yes, I see. However, I think you said that you live in Pennsylvania. Our residents' families always live nearby, certainly within a day's drive. Do you plan to relocate to Colorado yourself?"

Sidnei sat in silence for several seconds while she gathered her thoughts. "Well, actually no. My parents wouldn't be expecting my husband and I to be moving to Colorado. And both my husband and I work very well from our home."

"Hmmm … yes. How often do you think you would be visiting then? It will be important for you to be an active member of the care plan team."

Sidnei was starting to feel a little squeezed with this conversation. "Currently, we fly to Phoenix every four to six weeks, more often if the circumstances warrant it. Honestly, though, we were hoping to find a safe place for them so that our trips could be less frequent."

"I see. Our residents are looking for their loved ones more often than that."

Sidnei bit her lip at the mention of "loved ones." She wasn't exactly sure where she now or ever fit into her parents' list of "loved ones."

"You see, we're looking for a place where my parents can feel safe, as I said, and comfortable and secure. We'll be available to help with decision-making, but we can't always be there physically."

"I'll tell you what I'll do. I will send you one of our brochures and a list of our expectations. You can look everything over and then give us a call back."

"Okay. Thank you," said Sidnei and quickly hung up. She slumped in her chair and massaged her forehead. After a few minutes, she was ready for call number two. This call she began with a basic description of her parents' health status. At the end, she added that while she would be actively involved with decisions made regarding her parents' care, that participation would often be by phone, email, or text.

"Okay, dear. That's fine. You mentioned your parents' dementia. Let me just tell you a little bit about how we handle couples."

"Okay!" Sidnei's smile was returning.

"As the dementia accelerates in one or both of them, we may have to separate them. This, of course, will increase expenses."

"I understand," said Sidnei.

"Often, their behaviors can become very violent toward others. Of course, if one passed away, then we would provide grief counseling. That would be an additional expense."

Sidnei was no longer smiling. "All right. May I ask you to send me all the information that you think I would need?" She thanked the woman and ended the call.

Sidnei paced back and forth. She wondered why this had to be so difficult. Taking a deep breath, she sat back down, made a list of things she wanted to have explained, and dialed the number for the next skilled nursing facility.

The director of the third facility answered the phone with a friendly hello and a hope that the person on the other end of the line was having a good day.

Sidnei sat right up. "Thank you! I'm having an educational day." Sidnei explained her parents' status, her involvement, and the need for all of them to be comfortable with any new setting that might be chosen.

"Perfect, Ms. Jewell! Let me just tell you a few basic things then about our operation. Three medical doctors rotate through our facility. We have an RN assigned twenty-four hours a day who oversees all medical needs of our residents. For every eight residents, we have an aide assigned to look after their physical needs, which includes bathing, dressing, feeding, mobility, you name it."

"My parents have been pretty immobile for quite a while. They have pressure sores from sitting for long periods of time."

"One of our RNs specializes in treating these very issues."

"And falling? They do fall."

"The staff are all trained for this kind of thing. They, in turn, work with each individual resident to help them stay safe."

"And getting them up and active?"

"Again, our whole staff are constantly working on this. Plus, we have a full-time activities director who is dedicated to having each person as active and busy as possible."

"So how much time would you say the nurses, aides, and other staff spend with each individual resident every day?"

"Our staff are very committed to having every resident fully engaged. No one gets to really just sit and not engage. That includes staff and residents."

"Good! Good! My parents can be stubborn and surly at times ..."

"Say no more. We all have better days. We're here to make as many days as possible the best that they can be."

"And food? My dad won't eat chicken or fish."

"Ms. Jewell, we have a full-time nutritionist on staff. Each resident has an individual meal plan. Often, we have found that our residents have lost some sensory sensitivity in regard to food and taste, so we work with that too."

"Your place sounds ideal. Please send me all your information, and I'll be getting back to you very soon."

"We would be delighted to have your parents stay with us. Please give us a call back if you have more questions."

Sidnei sat back and breathed deeply. The conversation she just had made the next two calls go smoothly. She knew what to ask now.

Dark had begun to descend as she ended her last phone call. She walked outside and looked for the moon. It sat high in the sky, hanging like a sliver of a smile. Sidnei smiled, and her smile grew as Logan drove up the driveway. She had much to report.

After a long conversation sharing what she had learned with Logan, Sidnei sighed and stood to stretch. Turning to Logan, she said, "This is one of the most difficult things I've ever had to do. I'm doing it, but I find myself fighting it sometimes. What if someone doesn't have somebody to carry the ball for them? That's where I get stuck. I don't want to carry the ball here, but there's no one to pass it to. Does that make me a bad person?"

"I'm amazed at your tenacity with this whole situation. You're a good person, Sidnei. Don't ever doubt it. Your parents are in trouble. We're here. Your brothers have made it pretty clear that they're not going to help. As ugly as that is, this may be the best way. Heck! It's the only way," said Logan. He reached over and gave Sidnei a kiss.

"My family is a bad trip any way you size them up." Sidnei laid her head on Logan's shoulder.

"You have to remember you've always been able to weather their storms and stay out of the fray. It has made you one strong woman. And with that, I say we move on to another topic. Give us a new topic—like any word from the magazines? What do you say?" said Logan, making goofy eyes at Sidnei.

Sidnei reached for the mail and held up two envelopes. Her smile stretched from ear to ear. Logan grabbed her and gave her a big hug.

"And here's a kiss for my favorite photojournalist!" Logan gave her a long, lingering kiss.

Sidnei sighed. "Now if I can just make things right for my parents …"

"New topic, remember?" Logan crossed his arms and looked pointedly at Sidnei.

"Okay. You've got it," said Sidnei, though still turning back to her notes and her thoughts.

The one thing Sidnei knew her parents had given her growing up, albeit unknowingly, was a sense of security to be who she wanted to be. She wanted them to feel safe the remaining days of their lives. Yes, her parents were distant, secretive, and often not to be totally trusted, but damn it, they were her parents.

A couple of weeks later, Sidnei and Logan flew to Denver. Two and a half days of facility visits and conversations answering all their questions and concerns brought one facility to the forefront. It did not have an immediate opening, but both Sidnei and Logan knew that they needed lead time to make their case with Sidnei's parents. Further, the facility recommended a Denver attorney whom they trusted to help with drawing up a new will and making Sidnei the sole power of attorney for health and financial matters. Sidnei and Logan could now return to Phoenix armed not just with good intentions but also with good information to convince Sidnei's parents this was the best decision they could make for themselves.

24

The bare winter limbs of the trees cascading along each side of the waterfall were sheathed in fluffy white layers of soft, new fallen snow. Snowflakes danced in the frosty air. A wind was rising, and the voices of the ancients floated on the currents.

Sidnei snuggled into a familiar curve of the cave wall. She listened intently as the tinkling of chimes drew her attention to the front of the cave where swirls of snow marched to and fro from the corners of the falls forming an X shape. *Like a kiss*, thought Sidnei. The swirls, though, slowly appeared to take on unearthly shapes and forms. Sidnei sat up and rubbed her eyes as she caught a distinct chanting rolling in on the wind. Were her eyes deceiving her? Those surely were not angels' wings descending to a central point behind her waterfall. Yet there was no mistaking the light, feathery brush of wings across her shoulders.

There was someone lying down behind the center of the falls. Very seldom was anyone other than Logan with her in this place. And the walls and floor of the cave behind the waterfall were so very, very cold. A rush of wind and fog and mist colluded with the now distinct chanting. Muddled conversations surrounded the figure until a larger figure lumbered into the space. The shadowy figures retreated a few steps and allowed this new figure to grope for the figure on the ground. There was no mistaking this new figure when he directed those sightless, lifeless blue eyes toward the heavens and beseeched the heavenly powers.

"No! No! No! God, please no!" Then all went silent as the blinding whiteness gave way to stark darkness for a few moments.

Then the snowflakes began turning into icy crystals, blurring the images that slowly faded back into the heavens. The glow of the moon shone off the sparkling ribbons of the waterfall.

Sidnei found herself awake in her bed, shaken, frightened, and freezing. She bundled up in a robe and wandered out to her studio. The moon cast tendrils of light through the windows. Sidnei sat for a while just watching the moon and hugging her body. Then long, arched clouds sporting angels' wings slowly made their way by the moon, and Sidnei whispered, "Goodbye, Mom." Her tears slowly etched a path down her cheeks.

25

When the phone rang a couple of hours later, Sidnei caught it on the first ring. She needed only to respond with "yes" each time the stages of her mother's death were described. She had, after all, been in attendance. Her dad was nearly inconsolable when he was put on the phone. She thanked the fireman giving her the report and promised to call her dad back in about an hour.

Still chilled and rattled, Sidnei went to wake Logan. After Sidnei related all the events to Logan, he took her in his arms and squeezed tight. Then he held her a little away from him, looking her over carefully.

"This is probably the best thing that could happen for your mom. All this has to have been difficult for her. Maybe now she'll know some peace," said Logan.

"I know, but it continues to get freakier. And we were so close to getting her out of there," said Sidnei, a weariness in her voice.

"You know your dad can't stay there on his own now," said Logan.

"Maybe that was what we were doing the last several weeks, preparing to make it easier for him to make the transition," thought Sidnei out loud.

"Could be, could be," said Logan, looking at Sidnei with concern.

Sidnei's eyes wandered around the room. The images of her dream were still vivid in her mind, especially the gentle nudges from the angels. Was there a message in those nudges?

"I need to call Dad soon. He was pretty shaken up when I spoke with him earlier," said Sidnei, now returning Logan's gaze. "I'm just thinking how difficult it will be for him without Mom. She was always there," said Sidnei, her voice growing softer as her eyes filled up with tears.

Logan hugged her again and whispered into her ear, "You know I'll always love you and want you by my side, Sidnei Jewell."

Sidnei hugged him back extra tight, adding a kiss at the end. Then she announced, "And now I must make my phone call."

"I have a couple of things to take care of myself. I'll be in the next room if you need me," said Logan.

Sidnei made her call. She found her dad more centered, and thankfully more submissive when she informed him he would have to move. His only request was that he be close to her mom. This Sidnei could promise with certainty. She explained she would contact Randy to help her dad pack and to get him to the airport and checked in. With that information, her dad began to break down, and he passed the phone off.

Sidnei was surprised to hear Zelly's voice. "I am so sorry, Sidnei."

"Thank you," said Sidnei as she fought back tears. "I'm glad you're there. How is my dad doing do you think?"

"He's pretty broken up, I'm afraid. I'll stay with him for a while just to be sure there will be someone with him."

"You mean my brother isn't there? Who reported the death?"

"Well, I actually came by to check on your parents and found them both on the family room floor. Your dad was sitting behind your mom, cradling her head in his lap. I don't know how long he sat there with your mom. I called emergency right away. Your dad did say Garvan had not been around for several days."

Sidnei sighed a long, deep sigh. She swiped at her tears, which were quickly being taken over by anger. She paced as she spoke. "So, my brother doesn't know my mom has passed away?"

"No, he does not. I really don't know what to say."

"The fireman I spoke to earlier said they were going to do some tests."

"Oh, yes, they did do a drug screening but found nothing. In fact, they were a little alarmed because they knew your parents couldn't be doing well, and yet they couldn't find a single medication in the house. I am so, so sorry for all of this."

Sidnei took a few deep breaths before responding. "Did my mom suffer?"

"No, she did not. Your dad said your mom lay down on the floor to rest.

When he tried to wake her a little while later, he couldn't hear her breathing. Her heart just stopped beating."

Images from her dream came flooding back to Sidnei—her mom on the ground, the cold, cold floor behind the waterfall, her dad reaching out for her mom, the angels' touch. She caught her gasp as the tears fell.

"Sidnei, she did not suffer. She went to sleep and just never woke up."

"Thank you, thank you," said Sidnei. Her sigh was now a heavy one.

"The funeral home here has been notified, so you'll be getting a call from them soon. If there is any way I can help, please let me know. I think I should get back to your dad for now. You'll be in my thoughts and prayers."

"Thank you," said Sidnei as she sat down. With that call ended, Sidnei held her head in her hands and wept, asking herself over and over again, Was there no end to this misery? Her head ached, her shoulders ached, her back ached, her stomach ached, and her heart ached so badly she thought it might burst.

When Logan came into the room, he scooped Sidnei up in his arms and held her tight. When Sidnei's tears subsided, Logan shared that he had made all the flight arrangements. They would be meeting her dad at the Denver airport tomorrow evening. He had also spoken to the skilled nursing facility and learned that they did have a single room available. It was being made ready for her dad.

As Logan hugged Sidnei again, she could hear all the pieces beginning to fall into place—*clunk, clunk, clunk*. Leaving Logan, she called Randy, who immediately offered his condolences and added that he would personally take care of her dad. Sidnei explained that he would need to pack as many of her dad's things as possible since her dad would not be returning. That done, Sidnei alerted the restaurant that today would be the final day for food delivery. Two more pieces, *clunk, clunk*. The Phoenix mortuary called to say their provider in the Denver area was prepared to receive her mom, who was already in transit. *Clunk, clunk*. The pieces kept coming together, one by one, sliding into place to meet for the final rendezvous. Sidnei sat, closed her eyes, and fitfully rested as scenes of the past months rushed through her mind. Bigger pieces to a bigger picture? If only her heart didn't feel like it was tearing bit by bit.

She needed to walk. Walking always made everything clearer and brighter. Sidnei stood up and went in search of Logan.

Finding Logan, she said, "I need to go for a walk to clear my mind and my heart. Want to go with me?"

They walked together, side by side, for a couple of hours, each mostly lost in their own thoughts. Still pretty quiet, they arrived back home, packed, and were at the airport bright and early the next morning. When Sidnei's dad arrived at the Denver airport, they were there waiting to meet him. As he approached them in a wheelchair, his head hung over his lap, his body tensed, his nose dripping.

"Hi, Dad!" said Sidnei as she planted a kiss on his wet cheek. She quickly wiped his nose.

Logan patted his shoulder.

Sidnei's dad raised his head. He stared blankly ahead, the light gone from his eyes. "That you, Sidnei?" he asked flatly.

"Yes, it's me. I was sort of expecting to see Garvan with you," said Sidnei as she took over for the attendant.

"Haven't seen him in days," said her dad.

She looked alarmingly at Logan, who in turn, got on his cell phone. He quickly formed a zero with his thumb and forefinger and mouthed the words "Wiped out."

"Geez," said Sidnei under her breath. She knew her mom and dad's retirement monies had only been deposited earlier that day. Yes, while she and Logan were in flight, she thought. Well, never again. They would see to this before they returned home.

"Dad, let's get all the luggage and take you to your new home," said Sidnei brightly.

Sidnei and Logan made small talk with Sidnei's dad all the way to the skilled nursing facility. The staff there were welcoming and took over for Sidnei and Logan right away, sending them on their way. The two of them checked into their hotel, had a glass of wine, and called it a night, wrapped in each other's arms.

They were ready to start addressing issues after a good night's sleep and a hearty breakfast. The funeral was still two days away. Sidnei and Logan first made contact with the attorney they had been talking to in the Denver area. They were able to arrange a meeting to include the two of them, Sidnei's dad, and the attorney at the skilled nursing facility for the following day. This meeting would give Sidnei full power of attorney for all health and financial concerns for her dad. Next, they called their bank in Pennsylvania to set the steps in motion for the new accounts with all three of their names. Through email and fax, Sidnei was made the POA for the sale of her parents' home in Arizona. She agreed to go to Phoenix after the funeral to settle some things regarding the contents of her parents' home. Little by little, then by leaps and bounds, Garvan would be cut off. It wasn't guaranteed to be foolproof, but Sidnei and Logan were decidedly relieved. More pieces clunked into place.

The funeral directors had explained to Sidnei that they would take care of pretty much everything related to the funeral and burial. Sidnei knew this even included making arrangements for Mass to be said at the local Catholic church in Watkins. Thinking she should still check in, Sidnei called the funeral director in Denver to see how things were going. Not only were things under control, but this also included things Sidnei had not even thought about, like planning a luncheon for after the services. She did offer ideas about scriptures to be read and songs to be sung. After the conversation, she heaved a big sigh of relief. This was all a bit overwhelming, and she had to admit she needed the help of other people right now.

Although she had neither seen nor had much contact with her cousins in many years, they had quickly taken over informing the appropriate people to attend the funeral. It occurred to Sidnei that she was at a loss when faced with conjuring up a guest list. Her cousins were happy to help. In fact, it appeared this was a natural event for them. Sidnei couldn't remember the last funeral she had attended. Maybe she should take notes, she thought. This made her smile, something she realized she had not done spontaneously for a long time. The smile eased her heart.

With almost all the pieces falling into place, Sidnei felt her armor of discontent beginning to ease off her shoulders. The remaining blank pieces she needed to let go for a while. Logan waved to her from across the room while he took part in a work-related Skype conference call. She blew him a kiss, threw on her walking shoes, and walked the neighborhood surrounding their hotel. In the back of her mind was the soothing sound of her waterfall. Above her was a continuous flight of feathery clouds. The universe was in motion. Here on earth, traffic was light, but walkers and runners moved all about her. Life went about its business. When she returned to the hotel, two messages awaited her. Both announced publishing dates for her Iceland articles, the one on the northern lights in a national travel magazine, and the other article on the Icelandic horse in a popular equestrian magazine. She couldn't help but smile.

Later in the day, Sidnei and Logan drove out to Watkins. It had not changed at all. Asphalt paved a path straight through the town. Banged-up cars and rusting pickups were parked every which way in front of the few businesses open—a small grocery, a car repair shop with one gas pump available, a six-room motel and bar with a partially lit neon sign announcing it was open. A couple of other buildings were boarded up. Utility poles spanned the outlines of the town. An elementary school and two churches, one Catholic, the other Methodist, were nestled among houses with peeling paint, broken shutters, and yards blooming with weeds. Sidnei and Logan found the weeds carefully mowed at the cemetery located on a slight rise above the mean little town.

"You know, my dad was once offered a teaching and coaching job nearby," reflected Sidnei as she took in the desolate landscape.

"He didn't seriously consider it, did he? I can't see him, and especially your mom, hunkering in here," said Logan, also scanning the barren horizon.

"No, no! It was one of the few times my mom spoke up and said no," said Sidnei. "I had forgotten about that. She actually said no." Sidnei's voice trailed off as her thoughts raced.

Tumbleweeds rolled by their feet. The persistent wind chilled them. The work had been started for preparing her mother's grave, and this they found sobering. Sidnei found herself immersed in a silence reminiscent of those she grew up with. She could sense the old bones scattered around her trying to reach out and touch her. She shivered and reached for Logan's hand. Silently, the two of them returned to the car and drove to the skilled nursing facility.

They arrived to find Sidnei's dad disconsolate. He offered little except to say, "They washed and ironed all the clothes I brought. Said most of them were filthy. How can that be? Your mom kept everything immaculate," he said, hanging his head again.

Neither Sidnei nor Logan could get her dad to say anything after that. They quietly said goodbye and went to see the director, who greeted them with a warm smile.

"How are you two doing? The past months were certainly not easy for you." The director's smile had turned into a genuine look of concern.

"We're doing better than my dad. He's never very talkative when we're around, but today he's despondent." Sidnei looked perplexed and disturbed.

"I want you to know that under the circumstances, his behavior is pretty normal. He lost his wife of many, many years quite suddenly. He also isn't in the best of health himself. He needs to eat more to begin with, and that's exactly where we're beginning with him."

"So, I should relax a little, you're saying?" Sidnei could feel a smile starting.

"Yes, dear, that's what I'm suggesting. He's in very good hands here. We've looked over his clothes, and we're preparing his outfit for the funeral. We'll have him dressed appropriately, as he described your mother would expect him to dress."

Sidnei laughed at this. "My mom was always on his case about what he wore to church."

"We've heard the stories. We'll make her proud."

"Thank you!" Sidnei was warming up to this woman more and more.

"We can't promise, but we'll also try to make him a little more personable for your meeting with the attorney tomorrow. In getting to know him, we've found he can be quite charming."

All three of them laughed at this. Sidnei and Logan thanked the director and went on their way to enjoy a quiet evening.

When Sidnei and Logan returned the next day, they found her dad dressed in slacks and a polo shirt with coordinating socks and a smart pair of loafers on his feet. He was clean shaven, and his nails had been manicured. He looked like the dad Sidnei remembered from what seemed very long ago.

"Wow, Dad, you look great today! All ready for our meeting?"

"Humph! These people said I had to look sharp for this lawyer."

"Well, you do! Don't you think he looks good, Logan?"

"Sure do!"

"Anything in particular you want us to address with the attorney, Dad?"

"Nope. You're in charge now. That damn Garvan left me high and dry. Now you can use some of those smarts you were always bragging about."

Sidnei's dad shut down after this. The attorney arrived, shook hands, and got right to work. She came prepared. As they worked through each of the documents, Sidnei would turn to her dad and explain it to him. He would nod but not look up, asking only, "Where do I sign?" Sidnei guided his hand to the signature line, and her dad affixed his failing signature to each document.

As they came to the final documents, the attorney took off her glasses and turned to Sidnei's dad. "Mr. Jepson, you do understand that you're giving your daughter total control of your health and financial needs? You're giving away immense responsibilities."

"Yep. Came here to die. Now where do I sign?" Sidnei's dad had not looked up once since the meeting began. He sat hunched over the table, defeated.

Sidnei and the attorney looked at each other but said nothing.

"Just a few more things then, Mr. Jepson, and I'll be on my way. It sounds like your daughter may be bearing the brunt of the financial obligations here, so am I correct in assuming you'll want to be cremated to save a little money?"

Sidnei's dad raised his head, a faint glimmer of his old icy stare in his eyes. "I'm going to meet my wife the way she always knew me, whole, dressed in a coat and tie, going out in style, in a casket." His stare briefly focused on each one of them. Then he closed his mouth, hung his head, and wept.

Sidnei patted his back as the meeting finished up. The attorney was thanked, and Sidnei walked with her to the door. When she returned to her dad, he was unable to respond to anything she said. She gave him a hug, and Logan shook his hand. The director came to take Sidnei's dad back to his room and assured Sidnei and Logan he was going to be fine.

When Sidnei and Logan returned the next day to pick up Sidnei's dad for the funeral, he stood tall in his dress clothes to greet them with, "Jezzi was the only one, the only one, who stuck by me." This he would repeat throughout the day. At the church, he asked Sidnei how her mom looked. Sidnei said she was beautiful of course and surrounded by her favorite red roses. The scent of roses filled the air, and Sidnei's memories of her mom flew through her mind. She looked past her dad to catch Logan's eye. Logan mouthed "I love you" and sent her a wink.

Sidnei's dad clung to the two of them as they made their way to the front pew. Once seated, her dad reached for Sidnei's hand and wept openly. At the cemetery, he continued to hold Sidnei's hand while repeating, "The only one, the only one."

The wind blew tumbleweeds around them. The sky was dark with rapidly moving clouds shaped like angels' wings. Thunder could be heard in the background. Sidnei drew her coat about her while holding her dad's hand with one hand and Logan's with the other. These two men had shaped her life, one for better, one for worse. She felt the tears trickle down her cheeks.

Sidnei's dad grew quiet as people approached him at the reception. Sidnei made small talk with this group of mostly strangers while keeping a wary watch on her father. His blue eyes had lost all their light. He sat slumped, the fight no longer with him. Were there no more opportunities awaiting him? Sidnei wondered. Sidnei kept thinking, silently hoping, that one of her brothers might show. She had seen to it that her mom's obituary appeared in numerous newspapers. The absence of Sidnei's brothers was noted by all, often with distress and disbelief. All remembered how fond her parents had been of their boys. Sidnei remained by her father's side until the last guest had had their say and paid their final respects to him.

Sidnei and Logan said their farewells to her dad when they returned him to the skilled nursing facility. He accepted their hugs and Sidnei's kiss but said nothing. He sat shrunken, defeated, alone, and silent with his own private thoughts and demons. Exhausted, Sidnei shed no more tears, but she knew she would not soon forget this picture of her father.

The next morning, Sidnei and Logan flew from Denver on to Phoenix where they met with the Realtor. Good news awaited them, as a buyer was all ready to purchase the house for cash. The three of them quickly walked through Sidnei's parents' house, discussing how to best disperse of the contents. As they came back to the front door, a vehicle screeched to a stop outside. The front door was thrown open, and there was Garvan flailing the For Sale sign in his hands.

"You fucking cunt! What is this? This is my house!" Garvan moved a step closer.

Logan made a move to step between them, but Sidnei grabbed his arm and quietly said, "No, this is mine to handle."

Logan nodded his assent. Out of the corner of her eye, Sidnei saw he still had his phone out—ever ready, she assumed.

"Handle?" Garvan laughed a bone-chilling laugh.

"Clearly you're not capable of handling anything." Sidnei swept her eyes around the room, took another step forward, and put her hands on her hips.

"You, you ..." Garvan glared at Sidnei, but she didn't flinch.

"You *do* know our mother passed away." Sidnei's heart raced as a tear tried to escape.

"Sure. It was about time. The old lady had lost her friggin' mind. Couldn't even find her credit cards anymore. Now, out of my way." Garvan's face was red, his breathing labored.

"No, you need to be out of my way." Sidnei stood her ground. Neither she nor Garvan moved as she continued. "One, you have no right to speak of our mother like that. She doted on you. And for your information, I have all the credit cards. Two, I have power of attorney to sell the house, and it's sold. If you have anything inside, you need to take it now."

Garvan's eyes narrowed. He dropped the sign and clenched his fists. "I'll damn well get my stuff when I want to."

"I said the house is sold. It's now or never." Sidnei held her stare.

"Where's Dad?" Garvan now looked away. His eyes narrowed to slits.

"Safe and well cared for in Colorado. Near Mom." Sidnei caught the tears before they could fall, breathing deeply and evenly.

Garvan sneered. "So, when do I get my money from the sale of the house?"

Sidnei laughed. "And what money would that be? You already extorted all of Mom and Dad's money. They had three mortgages on this place. Their monthly payments were more than the house is worth. Good job, Garvan, not taking care of things for them. I think you need to leave." Sidnei's anger flashed in her eyes.

"What about the life insurance?" Garvan was shuffling his feet nervously.

Sidnei threw her head back and laughed deeply. "That was borrowed against also. You should know that, unless you're more ignorant than I've been thinking. I don't know what shady schemes you've been up to, but it's gone. It's all gone. I'll tell you nicely one more time. Leave." Sidnei swept her arm toward the front door.

Garvan smiled a smile Sidnei recognized too well. It was eerie, for she saw a younger version of her dad standing in front of her. She shook her head to get the image out of her mind.

"Well, how about gas money?" Garvan grinned.

"Have you no shame? Get out! Out!"

Garvan stomped on the sign and looked squarely at Sidnei. "Dad always said you thought you were too good for us. He really meant you're no damn good to any of us." Garvan stormed out the door, kicking everything in sight and cursing all the way to his truck. He drove the truck up on the curb and then turned it around violently. The truck turned the corner at a dangerously high speed. He was gone.

Sidnei turned to Logan and the Realtor. Tears streamed down her face. Logan held her with one arm while now holding his phone to his ear with the other arm. "So, you got all that, right? Okay. Thank you."

Sidnei looked up at him, confused. He put both arms around her now. "Just thought the police might want to listen in."

Hugging Logan tightly, Sidnei spoke breathlessly. "The police wanted proof. You gave it to them. You gave it to them." Months of tension fell off Sidnei's shoulders as she leaned deep into Logan's chest for a few minutes. Then she turned to the Realtor.

"I am so sorry you had to be a witness to that."

"Don't be. I'm a little worried he may be back though. He seemed rather aggressive." The Realtor was visibly shaken.

Sidnei looked at Logan as she said, "I don't think he'll be back any time soon."

The three of them sat quietly for a while until a patrol car pulled up to the house. The officer took their statements and promised to get back to them. Meanwhile, he suggested they lay low. He informed them that Garvan had a record, and it wasn't pretty. The three of them all agreed to go home. For Sidnei and Logan, that meant their peaceful country home in Pennsylvania.

For the first two weeks after they returned home, Sidnei's dreams were filled with repeats of major turning points in her life. Distant memories of her parents' fond attention until she was about four, moving, always moving, basking in the attention of people other than her parents, watching her parents, especially her dad, encourage and befriend other girls, and then learning she could come and go as she pleased because no one seemed to care. Was that because, as Garvan had suggested, she was no damn good to anyone? Was it because she was too smart? The dreams left her exhausted and out of sorts. Her photography and writing brought her out of her funk. She had to admit she was good at what she loved. The reviews of the Iceland articles alone assured Sidnei that she knew better. She was not only smart but also talented and loved. It was time to go for a walk.

She went for many walks the next couple of weeks. On these walks, she explored the neighboring fields and gathered wild seedlings for her gardens. And she kept her eye on the sun.

Then she received a call from the Phoenix Police Department. "Morning, Ms. Jewell. I'm Officer Rodriquez. I spoke to you at your parents' house a while back."

"Oh, yes, of course, Officer," said Sidnei, her brain going in many different directions.

"I have some news I thought you would want to hear."

"Yes?" Sidnei looked down to see she had crossed her fingers.

"Your brother Garvan has been intercepted at the border with Mexico. He's been charged with the trafficking of a dozen very young Hispanic women."

Sidnei knew she had been holding her breath, and she made a conscious effort to take a deep breath. "Are the young women all right?"

"They had been traveling for a long time, so they're tired and dirty, probably haven't eaten in a while. They're in good hands now."

"Thank goodness."

"Another thing. Garvan was in possession of several different narcotics, OxyContin, Vicodin, Demerol, Fentanyl. Seems they were still in their original prescription bottles."

"Did …" Sidnei could not speak. She shuddered as a chill ran up her spine.

"They all had your parents' names on them. I know when the fire department turned in the report after your mom's death, the fireman was a little suspicious about not finding any drugs in the home."

It was remarkable how still everything had become, Sidnei thought. "Thank you for letting me know," she said quietly as a vision of a phoenix rising up out of the ashes filled her head.

"I want you to know that your brother has been a person of interest for a while now. We can all sleep better tonight. You can take it easy now, ma'am."

Sidnei thanked him for the information and sat in her studio where she cried and cried and cried for hours after she hung up, a door banging and clunking repeatedly in the back recesses of her mind where the ashes slowly turned to dust. Odd how justice played out. That evening, Logan held her for a long time.

Sidnei called her dad the next day but kept the conversation light. Her dad did not ask about Garvan. In fact, he had not asked about him since the funeral. Sidnei didn't share the information about Garvan's capture. There was enough sadness in his world. She had so many questions, which she knew all too well would never be answered.

Several months later, Sidnei set her phone down, a smile on her face. She had just finished talking to the director of the skilled nursing facility who had reported that her dad was now settling in well. He had a few friends among the patients, whom he entertained with stories about his paths to opportunities. Strange that she was not familiar with most of the particulars of these stories that the director had shared. But then she knew they probably changed with each telling. It was like a shell game.

Sidnei still had not gone through the last box of her dad's files. Outside, the weather was drizzly and wet. Logan would be working late today. This just might be the day for her to attack that box. She pulled the box out of the closet where she had stored it. An espresso in hand, Sidnei settled into a comfortable chair and began to sort the various items. The small file marked

"Attorneys" inside the "Legal Transactions" folder drew her attention first. Many of the papers were yellowed with age. Not surprisingly, several had to do with Garvan's exploits, a few even with Tam's, but mostly the papers had to do with her dad. As she sorted these papers by date, her eyes were drawn to a date not easily forgotten. Her heart rate picked up. Her dad had abruptly left the only job he had known, that of teacher and coach, about this time. Her eyes grew wide; her mind began to race. Maybe the big "Why?" would be answered. Sidnei got up, prepared herself another espresso, and settled herself once again, kicking off her shoes and curling up in the chair. The document was only three pages long but held a lifetime of answers. Sidnei read it through twice as her breathing became irregular, her tears growing steadily.

Her father, she learned, had been implicated in various grooming schemes. Grooming she knew had something to do with luring kids into sexual acts. Surely not her dad. Everyone liked him. He helped kids. Well, didn't he? Sidnei moved to her computer. The general definition read, "Child grooming is befriending and establishing an emotional connection with a child, and sometimes the family, to lower the child's inhibitions with the objective of sexual abuse." Sidnei was growing sick to her stomach. The article continued, "Child grooming is also regularly used to lure minors into various illicit businesses, such as child trafficking, child prostitution ..." It went on. Sidnei closed her eyes. Pictures of her dad with all those cheerleaders, and later younger women who always looked very familiar, tumbled through her head. The envelopes of money given to her dad by strange men ... She got up to run to the bathroom to throw up.

Sidnei splashed cold water on her face and made herself breathe long, deep breaths. Returning to the computer with paper and pen in hand, she began to take notes. The legal definition was ominous. "In the U.S. child grooming is considered a federal offense pursuant to 18 USCS 2422, the provision of the section reads as (a) Whoever knowingly persuades, induces, entices, or coerces any individual to travel in interstate or foreign commerce, or in any Territory or Possession of the United States, to engage in prostitution, or in any sexual activity for which any person can be charged with a criminal offense, or attempts to do so, shall be fined under this title or imprisoned not more than 20 years, or both."

Her dad had been friends with everyone. That afforded him opportunities she had been unaware of apparently. Her dad helped his high school students and occasionally their families with bills and necessities. She had thought maybe they returned to thank him. Were those young women actually coming to the house to accuse him, to approach him? What? Her dad's mind was now trapped. She would never know the answers. The dirty little secrets would remain just that, dirty little secrets.

What did people really know about grooming in the sixties and seventies? A little more research said it had been a recognized crime since the 1920s. In fact, it had long been seen as a problem leading to the trafficking of women and children. The school district had been given her dad's name by a young woman found in a trafficking sting in Puerto Rico. She had stated a teacher and coach from her high school had put her in contact with the traffickers. Her dad had denied all the charges, but what was the truth? Her dad had always worked on getting the trust of high school students, particularly the girls, by giving them attention. His coaching gave him open opportunities to foster what appeared to be special connections. She carefully charted each move with each of her dad's new opportunities. Had these been calculated career moves or dismissals? There were a couple of other statements in the file, which hinted that the moves had been strongly suggested. In today's world, her dad would have made front-page news. Sidnei's nausea and despair had moved on to anger. And Garvan? The family business Aiden had alluded to?

Each allegation matched each move she had made as a young child. The final allegation suggested there was a victim who was prepared to come forward. If her dad relinquished his teaching certificate, agreed to leave teaching and coaching young kids forever, and moved himself out of the school district, the charges would not be pursued.

Sidnei took a deep breath as she reminded herself that that "opportunity" made it possible for her to meet Logan. As she gathered her thoughts, she thoughtfully went back over the definition for grooming. She sat back and visualized how many times she had observed her dad as an upstanding member within not only his school community but also the greater community where they lived. He was repeatedly recognized as that teacher and coach who was sincerely interested in the well-being of the young people with whom he worked and established trusting relationships with them. She had spent a lifetime trying to rise above the hurt she felt when she was shunned over and over again by both of her parents while she witnessed their generous overtures to other young people. Was her mom aware of all this?

Sidnei got up and began to pace. Was this the explanation for her increasing relegation as a person, as a female, as she grew older? After all, she had been a young girl with very little parental oversight herself. Anger simmered and festered, growing into a morass of feelings. All the painful moves, the scary silences, the mysterious envelopes, the curious liaisons, the avoidance of feelings and touch. Sidnei broke out into a loud sob as she realized why her mother had seldom really smiled. Her mom had to have known. Sidnei felt an overpowering sadness grab her heart. Drop by bitter drop, her blood grew cold. This went way beyond the mounting betrayal she had felt growing up.

Sidnei walked from room to room in her home. Her dad was old and tired. It seemed cruel to confront him. His dementia kept him trapped in confusion. Asking for an explanation would further confuse him and incite his anger. He probably would not miss seeing her if she chose not to visit. They had not, in fact, been close for many, many years. Yet she now had legal obligations for him and his well-being. The old tug-of-war between her heart and her mind reared up. She could not abandon her dad, nor could she condone his actions. She would see his needs were met, but her heart was hers alone to share with those whose love and integrity she admired. A peace, unlike any she had known before, settled over her.

Sidnei walked to the floor-length mirror in her bedroom. She looked at herself long and hard. As she made her assessment, she spoke out loud.

"Blonde curls laced with a few silver sparkles." Sidnei did a pirouette and then let her eyes rove.

"Trim figure, good mind, good heart, good wife, but good daughter?" She frowned and carefully studied her puzzled face.

"Accomplished in several spheres, appreciated by my community, liked by my friends for who I am, respected by my colleagues, loved by Logan." Here she stopped to smile at her reflection.

"But loyal to my family? What are the ties that bind me to my family?" She sat down in front of the mirror and crossed her legs.

"They did allow me to become my own person. But what of love, respect, the truth?" Sidnei had no tears left, nor would she allow any more to fall. She had seen to it that her dad would be safe. In large part, she now knew that meant safe from his past, a past she had known little about, but a past that was just that—past.

She stood up and stretched as far as her arms would reach. "I have a good life with a great love! I will move on. And I think I'll go for a walk." Sidnei skipped out the door humming an old familiar love song and smiled.

When Logan came home, Sidnei walked into his arms and stayed locked in his arms for a long, long time. When she stepped out of his safe embrace, she pointed to the file on the counter and the pile of notes beside it. "This is what Aiden and Tam knew and, I'm guessing, what Garvan's wife feared. They, no doubt, feared for their own children, maybe even for themselves. It should make me feel dirty, but I feel surprisingly free."

As Logan read, he looked up a couple of times, first in anguish and then in revelation. His eyes met Sidnei's.

"Sidnei, I am so sorry. Your home life was always a little off. In fact, it was downright weird at times, the way your parents let you run around without seeming to care. But this, well this … I really had no idea."

"I know. Me neither," said Sidnei quietly.

"What are you going to do?"

"I've thought about it most of the afternoon. He's my dad, and I've never been able to escape that fact. The fact that arises from these revelations is that he was suspected but never actually charged. He's alone but safe now. I'll pay the bills and make sure he gets what he needs. But he won't see much of me. I have to live the life we together have created, Logan." She smiled a slow smile.

"You've always been the most resilient person I've ever known. You're brilliant and beautiful and caring. I thought your whole family situation was incredibly odd at first, but you rose above it all. You made me try harder at everything. It wasn't too long after we started dating that I fell in love with you. Our crazy dates made anything seem possible. And this is so like you, just and fair and right. I love you more each day I know you, Sidnei Jewell."

With that, Logan pulled Sidnei toward him and wrapped her in his arms. There they stayed until the sunset captured their attention. They each grabbed a glass of wine and then sat in their deck chairs to take in the pure beauty of the sun setting behind their trees and before their lives. Slowly, the planets appeared, each in its rightful place, then the stars one by one, and the moon beamed above it all. Sidnei thought she heard her moon people sigh a contented sigh and laugh a gentle laugh. She smiled at Logan, the only man she had ever loved.